Cowboy for Eliza Jane

MAIL-ORDER BRIDES ON THE RUN, BOOK 3

JOVIE GRACE

ISBN: 978-1-63907-055-8

Get A Free Book!

Join my mailing list to be the first to know about new releases, free books, special discount prices, Bonus Content, and giveaways.

https://BookHip.com/LSPKMHZ

Acknowledgments

Thanks so much to my editor, Cathleen Weaver! Another big thank you goes to my beta readers, Mahasani and PigChevy. Last (but never least), I want to give a shout out to my Cuppa Jo Readers on Facebook. Thank you for reading and loving my books!

Chapter 1: Followed

ELIZA JANE

December, 1867

Eliza Jane Ferrell couldn't shake the feeling that she was being watched.

Glancing down the cobblestone street in front of her boarding house, she spied a scrawny orange cat giving her a hungry look. "Poor thing," she murmured, wishing she had a scrap of meat to toss his way. Unfortunately, she was hungry herself and too poor to do anything about it at the moment.

Her circumstances were about to change, though.

I hope. She smoothed her hands down the skirt of her black gown, quelling a shiver of apprehension that she quickly chalked up to bridal nerves. Her travel bag was already packed and resting on the ground at her feet. It contained everything she owned, which wasn't much — a nightgown, a few toiletries, and the Ferrell family Bible. The Bible contained a sketch of her wearing a ballgown drenched in lace. It was her only memoir of the life she'd once lived as a wealthy, indulged debutante.

Before the war had taken everything from her — her last living relative, her home, and her childhood sweetheart.

A piercing yowl from the emaciated cat drew her attention back to him. With one last glower in her direction, he finally gave up hope of receiving a handout from her and sidled on. Oddly enough, the feeling that she was being watched only grew stronger after he disappeared down an alley.

I'm probably imagining things. It was easy to do when a person was as hungry and exhausted as she was. It had been a long week, during which she'd lost count of the number of sewing and mending jobs she and her three boarding house roommates had taken in. Not to mention the endless loads of laundry and mountains of ironing. Her back and shoulders ached just thinking about it.

She was more than ready to trade in her life of drudgery in Atlanta to try her hand at ranching out west. According to her two other friends, who'd become mail-order brides a few months earlier, anything was better than working their fingers to the bone for the rest of their days. There was simply no getting ahead with this kind of work. It didn't pay enough.

Gazing from right to left, she knew with sudden certainty she wasn't going to miss these overcrowded city streets. The noise made her head throb, and the threat of danger around every corner kept her constantly looking over her shoulder. Over the past several days, a new worry had started to fester inside her concerning the safety of the three friends she would be leaving behind. They'd grown up together and always had each other's backs. After she left town, however, there'd be one less set of eyes watching the backs of the remaining three.

All four of them were impoverished southern belles. They'd descended from riches to rags together after the war. Despite that dismal fact, if she'd been a fly on the wall inside of the tiny, cramped boarding house room they shared, she would witness no envy or bitterness over her pending departure. Her friends were too busy donning their best hats and gowns to escort her to the train station. That's just how they were — always making the most of each tiny drop of sunshine that landed on their otherwise dreary existence.

Please, Lord, help them find husbands, too. Eliza Jane squeezed her eyelids shut and silently added one more request to her prayer. *In the same town, if it's not asking too much.* Good heavens, but that would be a dream come true! The very thought of having all six childhood friends reunited again was enough to take her breath away. Of course, that would require her remaining three friends to sign mail-order bride contracts like she had done, something they'd been reluctant to do up to this point.

There was a time when Eliza Jane had shared their sentiments about such a non-traditional means of securing a husband. A few years ago, none of them had pictured falling so far from their hallowed positions as high society debutantes. Quite the contrary. They'd anticipated making advantageous matches with the most eligible bachelors in town.

But that was then, and this was now.

Times had changed.

Fortunes had been reversed.

Their worst fears had been realized, and no distant relatives had stepped forward to offer a lick of charity.

Even then, Eliza Jane hadn't changed her opinion on the topic of becoming a mail-order bride until both Annabelle and Penelope had written from Texas. They'd insisted they were happy with the marriages The Western Moon Agency had placed them in. Annabelle even had a babe on the way!

Eliza Jane wasn't expecting to find quite that level of happiness in her own mail-order marriage. She was pretty sure that part of her heart had died with the beau who hadn't returned home to her after the war. However, she would be more than content with a roof over her head that wasn't contingent on meeting her next rent payment. She'd be mighty grateful for regular meals again, too. Her stomach gave a growl of hunger at the prospect.

She quickly forced her thoughts back to the train ride ahead. The envelope clasped in her hand contained a one-way ticket to El Gato, Texas. Upon her arrival, she would take a stagecoach the rest of the way to El Vaquero, a growing cattle town where a rancher named Keegan Ford was waiting to marry her.

They'd been corresponding by mail through the bridal agency — or rather through the law firm downtown that was representing them by proxy. She hoped with all her might that her groom-to-be would live up to the humorous, and even mildly sarcastic, version of him who'd been sending her letters.

A faint scratching sound to her left made her eyelids pop open again. Thinking the stray cat had returned, she turned her head toward the sound and stood riveted at the strange scene unfolding beside her.

A long string was slowly being lowered from the boarding house roof. Tied to the end of it was a rusty hook. Unless she was mistaken, the holder of the rope was lowering it directly toward the handles of her faded black travel bag.

They were trying to steal it!

Eliza Jane lurched into motion, snatching up her bag and shading her eyes with one hand to see who in tarnation would do such a thing.

A street urchin leered mockingly down at her. "Ya don' need it where yer goin', lady." His clothing was so tattered, and so much grime covered his face that it was impossible to tell his age. He was young, though. If he had a proper home, he would likely still be in school.

"I beg your pardon." Her heart sank the way it always did when she encountered one of the many homeless youths roaming the city. "I most certainly do need it, you little scamp!"

The urchin's dusty eyebrows rose. "In a brothel?" His voice rose to an incredulous squeak.

"A brothel!" What a strange thing for a child to say!

"Aye!" He eyed her pityingly. "The new one out west where yer goin'."

Alarm twanged through her at his words. It was clear to any onlooker that she was traveling, but how had he known she was heading west?

"How long have you been following me?" she demanded, glancing swiftly around them. She was all too aware that the street urchins downtown tended to run in packs. It was unlikely he was alone.

"Doesn't matter." The lad crept to the edge of the roof and crouched to spring down. His gaze was snapping with a curious brand of intensity. Though the local street gangs were notorious for pick-pocketing any and every person who happened to pass by, this particular encounter didn't feel random. He was deliberately stalking her.

"Who's paying you to do this?" She took a step back and reached for the doorknob leading inside. Since she'd never before laid eyes on the lad, whatever he was up to wasn't personal.

Instead of answering, he sprang over the eaves, his feet scissoring in her direction.

She twisted open the door to her boarding house room, jumped backward across the threshold, and slammed it shut behind her.

The street urchin's feet slammed into the other side of it while she was locking it. Dropping her travel bag, she whirled around to meet the startled faces of her friends.

Magnolia had been in the process of tying a bow in Emmaline's hair, as fiery red as her own thick, wavy tresses. She dropped her hands to her sides. "What in the world?"

"We have company," Eliza Jane explained breathlessly, pressing herself against the wall and leaning forward to peek out the only window in the room.

"Careful," Emmaline warned, pointing. Her pale, freckled features were twisted in horror.

A split second later, a stone crashed through the glass, shattering a large section of it.

Olivia Joy, who was normally the quietest one in their tight circle of friends, reached for the broom in the far corner of the room. Brandishing the handle like a general wielding a sword, she threatened in a voice Eliza Jane had never heard her use before, "Don't make us come out there! We're armed and dangerous!"

"We are?" Eliza Jane mouthed to Magnolia and Emmaline. Though Magnolia was a year older, the sisters looked enough alike in their matching bluebonnet wool dresses to pass as twins.

The three of them blinked in astonishment at their tiny, whip-thin friend. Her blonde hair was pulled back in a simple twist, and her faded green ballgown had seen better days. They watched as she reached for a mop on her way to the window, wielding the two cleaning tools with the same ferocity as if they were loaded guns.

"Who's out there?" Magnolia's voice was hushed as she spun her head in search of more weapons.

"A filthy little street urchin trying to steal my travel bag." Eliza Jane gave her a quick recap. "He lowered a fishing line from the roof to take it. When I caught him in the act, he leaped on top of me." She shivered. "Or tried to. I made it to safety first."

"I wonder if this is because of Penelope," Emmaline moaned,

twisting her hands in agitation in front of her. Only four short months ago, Penelope had been one of their roommates, but she'd signed a mail-order bride contract to escape the persecution of one of the largest street gangs in the city. They'd ruthlessly targeted her for the number of thefts she'd prevented in the park across the street from the boarding house — enough, they'd claimed, to put a significant dent in their ill-gotten profits.

"You think they're exacting their revenge on us in her absence?" her sister asked in surprise.

"Well, why else would they be after us?" Emmaline's voice trembled.

"I don't know," Eliza Jane cut in quickly. "Whatever it is, though, didn't sound like it had anything to do with Annabelle." Like Magnolia, Eliza Jane was scouring the room for anything she could use to defend herself. "In so many words, that little scamp called me foolish for not letting him have my travel bag. He claimed I didn't need it where I was going."

Olivia Joy's head jerked in her direction. "He knows where you're going? How?"

"I wish I knew." Eliza Jane blew out a frustrated breath. "He said something about a new brothel out west and seemed to be under the impression that's where I'm heading."

"A brothel!" Magnolia's sapphire blue eyes grew wide with incredulity.

"Maybe he mistook me for someone else." A shiver of apprehension worked its way across Eliza Jane's shoulder blades. "He was very bold and deliberate in his pursuit of me, though." For the life of her, she couldn't fathom who would pay anyone to track a poor, working-class girl like herself. She had no enemies she was aware of. She had no outstanding debts for anyone to collect. She owned nothing of value that could be resold.

A second stone crashed through the window, making all

four women jump. More of the glass pane shattered, sending shards flying in all directions.

"This is bad," Emmaline muttered nervously. "What are we going to do?"

"We'll get through it," Olivia Joy assured in a tight voice. "We always do."

"Will we?" Tears flooded Emmaline's eyes. "We got through things when there were six of us living together. Then five. Then four." She slowly shook her head. "But when Eliza Jane boards her train, there will only be three of us left." She shook her head. "I was already petrified about how much harder it's going to be to make our rent payment. But this?" She glanced pointedly toward the broken window. "We can't live this way. We just can't!"

A third stone grazed the wall over the window and clattered to the cobblestones below.

"You know we're going to be blamed for the broken window," she added shakily. "If we cannot come up with the money to replace it, our landlord will surely pitch us into the street."

A stunned silence met her words.

Eliza Jane tried to think of something comforting to say, but nothing came to mind. Emmaline was right.

"Maybe you should start packing." She spoke through stiff lips, unable to come up with any other solution.

"And go where?" Emmaline cried in piteous tones.

"To Texas with me," Eliza Jane said firmly. "The train doesn't depart for a few more hours."

"We can't even afford to replace the window!" Magnolia rounded on her, white-faced. "That means purchasing three more train tickets is out of the question."

"What she's trying to say is we should become mail-order brides like her." Olivia Joy grimaced as she faced the window again, bracing for the next attack.

"Mercy!" Magnolia's voice was barely above a whisper. It was as if all the energy had drained out of her.

"Do you have any better ideas?" Eliza Jane hated the fact that her last conversation with her friends was fast degenerating into an argument.

A fourth stone sailed through the gaping hole in the window. A burning rag was wrapped around it.

The four women watched in disbelief as it landed on Eliza Jane's bed and quickly ignited the linens.

"Fire!" Emmaline yanked a pillow off her own bed to bat at the flames.

Her efforts were of no use. The flames quickly spread to the mattress.

"Pack," Eliza Jane repeated firmly. She picked up her travel bag and reached for the deadbolt on the door. "We're almost out of time."

"She's right." Olivia Joy sprang into action, nearly tripping on the hem of her gown in her haste. She propped the mop and broom against the wall as she dug her travel bag from beneath her bed. "Grab what you can and let's go!"

The hands of her friends blurred from the speed with which they packed their few belongings. The smoke grew thicker and blanketed the room, making it harder for Eliza Jane to see anything clearly.

Pressing a sleeve against her mouth and nose, she coughed frenziedly against her arm. She lowered her arm for only the briefest of moments to yell hoarsely, "Are you ready?"

When no one answered, she reached for the broom Olivia Joy had left propped against the wall. "On the count of three," she bellowed, "I'm going to open the door." It was either that or stay inside and burn to death. She was already bracing herself for the distinct possibility they might have to fight their way out of the room.

"One! Two! Three!" She unlatched the door and yanked it

open. A cold, December breeze swirled into the room, making the flames on the bed leap higher.

She lurched across the threshold, waving the broom handle viciously back and forth to clear a path. To her relief, she met no resistance. Glancing over her shoulder, she was enormously grateful to see her friends spill out of the boarding house room behind her.

Olivia Joy had her travel bag in one hand and the mop in the other. Magnolia was clutching her travel bag and an empty silver wash bucket. Emmaline held a knobby, rolled-up blanket beneath her left arm with a sash tying it together. She was white-knuckling a washboard in her right hand. The four friends took off at a run down the cobblestone street, fanning out a little behind Eliza Jane.

Several passers-by stopped to gawk at them.

"Fire!" Shouts behind the women alerted them to the fact that the rising smoke from their boarding house room had finally been noticed. For once, Eliza Jane didn't bother looking over her shoulder. She was too busy watching for any sign of the street urchin who'd attacked her.

A team of horses clip-clopped up the street to their left, quickly gaining on them. The driver pulled abreast of her, slowing his horses so he could lean over and shout, "Climb aboard, and I'll give you a lift!" The door to the stagecoach swung open invitingly.

"Oh, thank you," Emmaline wheezed, slowing her speed. The bow her sister had tied into her hair earlier was drooping like a wilted flower.

Eliza Jane's gaze narrowed on the open door and fastened on a pair of women inside the coach. Despite the winter chill in the air, both were wearing scarlet red gowns with plunging necklines. They were no ladies. Their scandalous choice of apparel made Eliza Jane's fevered brain recall the street urchin's warning about the new brothel out west.

"Keep running!" She moved to the outer edge of their group, using her shoulder to nudge Emmaline away from the stagecoach. In the brief moment that she lifted her gaze from the street, she missed seeing a loose cobblestone and stumbled.

The two women inside the stagecoach took advantage of her momentary loss in equilibrium to reach for her. One clasped her shoulder. The other woman managed to wrap her fingers around Eliza Jane's wrist.

With a scream of sheer rage, Olivia Joy swung her mop toward the backside of the nearest horse, administering a swat to his right flank. He whinnied in fright and tried to rear back on his hind legs. It proved to be an impossible maneuver since he was hitched to three other horses. His frenzied movements ended up spooking the rest of the team, though, and sent them into a full gallop.

The two women in red struggled to maintain their hold on Eliza Jane, dragging her alongside the carriage for a few seconds. With an indignant gasp, Magnolia tossed her wash bucket in their direction, bopping one of the women hard enough on the side of the head to make her lose her grip. Eliza Jane managed to wiggle her wrist free from the other woman before losing her footing entirely.

The runaway horses quickly galloped the stagecoach out of sight. Eliza Jane and her friends huddled together, panting heavily and glancing wildly around them.

"Good gracious!" Magnolia shook her head in derision as a youth dressed in rags dashed into the street. He swept up her rolling wash bucket and took off with it like he'd struck gold.

"Let's keep moving," Eliza Jane urged tersely. Instead of heading straight for the train station as they'd planned at the start of their morning, she led them on a short detour to the red brick storefront that housed J. R. Hubert & Sons. It was the local law office acting in proxy for The Western Moon Agency in Texas.

Hettie Goodwin's familiar face appeared on the other side of the glass door. Her spectacles were balanced on the end of her slightly pointed nose as she held it open. The head secretary glanced in astonishment at the panting ladies trooping behind Eliza Jane into the room.

She pressed a hand to the throat of her navy, high-neck gown. Eliza Jane had yet to see her wear anything else.

"Well, I'll be!" She gave a curious sniff, no doubt smelling the trail of smoke and fear they'd left in their wake. She eyed the perspiration beading their foreheads and the bedraggled state of their hair and clothing. "I reckon there's an explanation for this...unexpected parade?" Shutting the door behind them, she fluttered her bony hands at them.

"I was attacked!" Eliza Jane was still trying to catch her breath. "Outside our boarding house room right before we departed for the train station." She drew in a bracing mouthful of air before continuing. "I ran back inside and bolted the door. That's when the next round of trouble began." She described the rocks that had come flying through their window, and the fire that had ensued.

"How awful!" Hettie's severe expression grew troubled. "Are any of you hurt?" Her gaze roved them again more slowly, assessing the small rips in the hems of their gowns.

The four friends shot questioning glances at each other and slowly shook their heads.

"No, but we can't go back." The first to recover her aplomb, Olivia Joy set down her travel bag and stood in the middle of the room. She gripped the mop handle like Moses preparing to part the Red Sea.

"Of course, you cannot!" Hettie looked horrified at the thought. "It isn't safe." She moved behind her desk and took a seat in her leather swivel chair. "Most unfortunately, I'm fresh out of quick and easy solutions to your problem." She spread her hands to gesture at the piles of paper on her desk. "Every last penny of the funds I have at my disposal is earmarked for transporting mail-order brides west."

Magnolia reached for Emmaline's hand. They exchanged a long, emotion-charged glance. "We'll do it," she declared softly. "If there is any way you can send my sister and me to the same town, we'd be much obliged."

Eliza Jane nearly choked on her tongue. "What she meant to say is we'd *all* like to go to the same town," she corrected firmly. "According to our friends in El Vaquero, there are plenty more marriageable men there."

"Be that as it may," Hettie pushed her spectacles higher on her nose to peer more closely at Eliza Jane, "what you're asking for is highly out of the ordinary." She blinked a few times. "Sending six mail-order brides from the same city to the same new town is, well...it's just not done!"

"Why not?" Olivia Joy gripped her mop handle more firmly, spreading her feet a little. "It's not as if we're asking you to do something illegal."

"Well, no." She vaguely waved a hand, looking like she was about to raise another protest.

"Nor would it be unprofitable for your firm." Eliza Jane imagined J.R. Hubert & Sons would earn the same finder's fee no matter where the head secretary sent her and her friends. Her mind spun dizzily at the thought of having all of her childhood friends reunited so soon. Up until this very moment, it had been no more than a castle in the clouds. However, Hettie Goodwin had the power to make it happen. Today. Right now, in fact.

Hettie's lips twitched as she surveyed Eliza Jane's hopeful expression. "We'd make a generous sum indeed if we succeeded in placing four more brides in El Vaquero instead of one. It's not easy finding marriageable young ladies willing to relocate to such a remote mountain community."

"Well?" Eliza Jane tapped the toe of her boot impatiently, wondering why the woman wasn't rushing to draw up three additional mail-order bride contracts. The clock was ticking.

Hettie seemed to be fighting an inward battle with herself. It ended when she drew a resigned breath. "What you are asking me to do is extraordinary, but not impossible." She abruptly stood. "It will require the approval, mind you, of the agency we represent. Since time is of the essence, please excuse me while I pay a quick visit to the telegraph office." Opening her center desk drawer, she withdrew the tiniest handgun Eliza Jane had ever laid eyes on. She motioned for her to take it. "In the event you were followed here by any of those hoodlums you spoke of, you'll want to be armed with more than a mop and a broom."

Eliza Jane silently accepted the gun. It felt strangely heavy in her hands. She hoped she'd never have cause to use it.

Hettie lifted her skirt and swept toward the front door. "Make yourselves comfortable." She nodded at the cozy seating area on the side of the room. "I made tea, and there's a tray of sweets on the coffee table."

Eliza Jane cast a longing look toward the tray of sweets. Her parting gift to her friends had been leaving her meager rations to them for the past day and a half.

"Go on now! Wash up and eat!" After delivering that final admonition, Hettie disappeared through the door, locking it behind her.

The moment the lock clicked into place, Eliza Jane and her friends dashed for the coffee table. By the time the secretary returned, the pot of tea was bone dry, and the tray of cookies had nothing but crumbs remaining on it.

They glanced sheepishly up from the circle of chairs they'd been perched on.

However, Hettie didn't so much as glance at the empty tray. "I have good news, ladies." A smile lit her stern features.

"As it turns out, exactly three more cowboys in El Vaquero are ready to get married."

Eliza Jane's shoulders sagged in relief. "Three more are all we need." She glanced around at her friends, taking in the varying degrees of anxiety straining their features. "Oh, come on," she protested, wondering why they didn't look happier at the news. "This is an answer to our prayers, and you know it!"

"We'll see." Olivia Joy smoothed her hands over her wind-blown hair, tucking a stray ringlet back into place. "Once upon a time, my prayers about my future husband included a very long list of attributes." Her delicate features momentarily dimmed with nostalgia.

"I can only imagine!" Hettie nodded in understanding. No doubt she was accustomed to doing business with young women who'd reached the end of their rope. "There's one thing I can do for you ladies that might make this whole process rest easier on your hearts."

Eliza Jane appreciated her choice of words and the kindness behind them.

Magnolia and Emmaline reached for each other's hands again while they waited for her to continue.

The secretary waved a small piece of paper in the air at them. "This telegram contains the three names of the three men who wish to be wed to you. Though The Western Moon Agency will have the final say in these matches, there's no reason you can't place your vote here and now for the cowboy you think will suit you the best."

Magnolia's mouth fell open on a breathless titter. "I'm a singer," she volunteered. "So is my sister."

Hettie pursed her lips as she took a seat behind her desk once again. "Then one of you might ought to marry the town minister. The reverend's name is Bo Stanley. I understand he's a mountain man who dresses a bit on the rugged side with a coonskin cap. He might require a little spit and polish, if you know what I mean." She glanced questioningly at the sisters over the top of her spectacles.

Magnolia raised and lowered her shoulders. "If he's truly a man of the cloth, how rugged can he be?"

"It's the wild west we're talking about," Emmaline reminded with a shiver. "I hear they're all a little rough around the edges in that part of the country."

Olivia Joy shifted her weight in her seat, looking impatient. "If no one else wants the mountain man, I'll marry him." Her voice was emphatic. "I'm certainly not opposed to being a minister's wife."

Hettie Goodwin dipped her pen in her ink bottle. "Then he's all yours, Miss er..." She arched her eyebrows at Olivia Joy.

"Olivia Joy Banks, ma'am."

Hettie started to write. "The other cowboys in need of wives are two more of the Ford brothers. Your friend Penelope married the oldest, most serious one, Jameson. Eliza Jane is to marry the second oldest one. Keegan is a bit of a jokester, but I've been assured he's hardworking and loyal." She continued writing. "The next two younger brothers are Carlton and Redding. Both are range riders, a job that requires long hours in the saddle. From what I understand, the Fords are working from sunup to sundown to round up all the wild longhorns in the area."

Magnolia exchanged a tremulous smile with Emmaline. "Two brothers for two sisters," she murmured. "I rather like the sound of that."

Eliza Jane only half-listened to their chatter. Her overactive imagination was back to fretting about why anyone would want her sent to a brothel — badly enough to set her boarding room on fire, then attempt to snatch her off the street in broad daylight.

Another thought struck her, one that was even more troubling. The man who'd offered her a ride in his carriage had extended his offer to her three friends as well. Had they accepted it, all four of them might very well be en route to that horrid place right now!

Olivia Joy caught her gaze. "I know what you're thinking." She spoke in undertones so the Dixon sisters couldn't hear what she said.

"Do you?" Eliza Jane was glad she was making an effort not to alarm Magnolia and Emmaline all over again, now that they were finally calming down about the notion of signing mail-order bride contracts.

"Yes. You're still worried about what happened earlier, and so am I. That said, I'm convinced the good Lord isn't going to let any harm come our way." Olivia Joy gave a decided nod. "Not so long as we continue to stick together. He gave us each other. That's how we've made it this far. Let's not ever lose sight of that."

Though Eliza Jane hoped she was right, she still couldn't shake the sense that whatever trouble was rumbling their way was far from over.

Chapter 2: Get Me to the Church

KEEGAN

Two weeks later

Keegan Ford opened the antique watch he'd inherited from his late father, glanced at the time, and closed it with a metallic snapping sound.

"By all that is great and good!" Jameson sent a light punch to Keegan's shoulder as he paced across the platform of the El Gato train station. "Put that thing away. The train isn't late. We got here early, is all."

Keegan continued to stalk back and forth past his oldest brother. It was his wedding day, so he felt as restless as a frog in a bed of rattlesnakes. However, he wasn't about to admit it aloud in front of his brothers.

Instead, he pushed back his Stetson and announced loftily, "I have every right to be concerned. According to The Western Moon Agency, someone tried to kidnap my bride-to-be on her way here."

"No doubt they wanted to get their hands on my lovely southern belle, as well," Carlton chimed in, looking more smug than worried. He possessed a competitive streak a mile wide. All the brothers did, but he'd been endowed with an extra wide streak of it. This morning, he seemed particularly tickled by the prospect of getting married on the same day as his next older brother, who was a full two years his senior.

"Mine, too." Redding jumped into the conversation, not one to be left out. He'd turned twenty-one only a month earlier, and their mother was far from thrilled about him marrying so soon. However, there'd been some mix-up with the agency that made little sense to Keegan. The result was that a few extra brides were heading their way, and Redding was next in line to snag one of them.

So was Reverend Bo Stanley.

Keegan almost chuckled at the way his best friend was tapping the toe of one enormous boot against the base of an unlit light pole. The tall beast of a mountain man was clearly as nervous as he was about meeting his new bride. Unfortunately, he didn't have Keegan's years of experience masking his feelings from a whole pack of brothers. He was wearing his anxiety right out in the open for all to see. Though it was the first week in December, his high forehead prickled with moisture. For once, though, he'd left his coonskin cap in the parsonage adjoining the church. In its place was a brand new brown felt Stetson.

It was possible he'd sought wardrobe advice from one of the womenfolk at Ford Ranch, because he was wearing new denim trousers and new leather boots. However, his resemblance to the Ford brothers stopped there. Instead of the dress shirts and suit jackets they had on over their trousers, he'd donned his favorite fringed deerskin coat. Though he'd trimmed his bushy reddish-brown hair and beard, he'd left a good two inches hanging from his jaw. He'd also kept his sideburns intact. From the side, the fellow could've passed for an enormous grizzly bear.

The Ford brothers were by no means short men, but they

were a few inches shorter than their mammoth mountain minister. And their Spanish heritage was proudly displayed in their dark eyes, brown hair, and bronze skin.

Keegan glanced over at the U.S. Marshal, whom he'd personally requested meet them at the depot. *In the event of any more trouble dogging our brides.* He genuinely hoped the lawman's intervention wouldn't be required today, but he'd rather be safe than sorry.

"Have you dug up any more news about that new brothel, marshal?"

Turner King shook his head, looking grim. "Not much." A man in his forties or thereabouts, the brothers knew very little about him — whether he was married or had any kin. He was a man of few words who showed up when he was needed and otherwise stayed out of their business. This morning, he was wearing all black, from his overcoat to his boots. His top hat and even his rifle were black. The only splash of color on his person was the gold star pinned over his heart.

"Not much implies that there *is* something," Keegan pressed.

The marshal shrugged. "It's your wedding day. Are you sure you want anything else to worry about?"

The man had new information alright. Keegan shrugged, not wanting to appear too eager. Sometimes, the marshal kept his cards pretty close to his chest. "Seems to me it'll be easier to protect my bride if I have all the facts."

"Have it your way," Turner King sighed.

"He usually does," Carlton muttered beneath his breath, shooting his brother a mildly antagonistic look.

Keegan ignored him. Now wasn't the time for a spitting match.

The marshal rocked back on his heels. "There's a mail-order bride agency in Savannah claiming they can't account for the whereabouts of two brides they sent this way."

Keegan didn't like the sound of that one bit. "You mean to El Gato?"

"Yes. The would-be grooms have confirmed the story."

"That would certainly lend credence to the rumors about a new brothel in the area." Keegan mulled over this latest bit of information, wondering why he hadn't heard any chatter about it from the locals.

"Still sounds like a whole lot of *maybes* and *ifs* to me," his oldest brother noted cautiously.

"But if there *is* any truth to it," Keegan pressed stubbornly, "they appear to be targeting young women in the south."

"Mail-order brides, to be more specific." Carlton's usual level of mockery was gone. The marshal's revelation about the missing women had visibly unnerved him.

"I think Turner King had the right of it when he suggested y'all just focus on your wedding day," Jameson countered in his calmest, older-brother voice. "How about we all take a step back, let him do his job, and only worry about this brothel business if he gives us a good reason to?"

"You just gave us another *if*," Carlton noted without humor.

Though Keegan knew their oldest brother was only trying to be reassuring, he resented Jameson's naivety in assuming there might be nothing sinister in play. *Good gravy!* Everyone and his dog knew that if Jameson's wife's safety had been in question, he'd be singing a very different tune. Jameson acted like the sun rose and set in Penelope Ford.

Instead of calling him out on his hypocrisy, Keegan merely asked the most burning question on his mind. "Why would anyone be targeting impoverished southern belles to fill a brothel?"

Turner King's gaze glinted with thinly suppressed anger.

"Other than the fact that they're beautiful, talented, educated, and well-mannered? I'll let you connect the dots."

The marshal's ready answer sent a blast of coldness through Keegan's chest. Clearly, the man had given the question some thought long before Keegan had asked it. "Sounds to me like your gut is telling you there's something to those rumors," he noted, not really expecting the man to answer.

The marshal spread his hands. "I have two missing brides and one attempted kidnapping on my hands. In my experience, that's too much to be a coincidence."

The distant hoot of a whistle alerted them to the fact that a train was about to enter the station.

Keegan shaded his eyes against the morning sunlight, but the train was still too far away to see. "Is there anything we can do to help with the investigation?" Out of the corner of his eye, he saw Jameson's shoulders stiffen at the question.

"What I need more than anything right now is for y'all to keep your brides safe." The marshal tightened his grip on the rifle propped against his shoulder. "The tighter the leash, the less work it'll be on me."

Keegan wasn't thrilled about the man's choice of words. Women weren't dogs to be kept on leashes. However, he agreed with the first part of what he'd said. "We'll keep them safe, marshal." He was relieved to see the train chug into view. As it coasted to the station, the brothers' hands automatically moved to the guns in their holsters. Making a few hand signals to communicate their intentions to each other, they took their pre-agreed-upon positions around the platform.

It had grown more crowded in the last few minutes. Family members were thronging both the top of the platform and the base of the steps now. A stagecoach and two other wagons were pulled against the curb of the street below.

Though Keegan's bride-to-be and her three friends had originally planned on hailing a stagecoach and riding it the rest of the way to El Vaquero, he and his brothers couldn't in good conscience allow them to. Not with the current threat hanging over their heads.

From the moment he'd signed his side of the marriage contract, Keegan had felt responsible for his mail-order bride's safety and well-being.

Eliza Jane Ferrell. Soon to be Eliza Jane Ford. He repeated her name in his head, very much liking the married version of it. He'd spent the last few weeks hoping and praying her personality would live up to the sassy tone in her letters. The last thing he wanted was to spend the rest of his life bored out of his mind.

He much preferred the idea of being married to a woman with a backbone. It was perfectly alright with him if she turned out to be easy on the eyes, too. He replayed Turner King's summation of southern belles inside his head. *Beautiful, talented, educated, and well mannered.* If his wife was all of those things, he'd be a fortunate man indeed!

Eliza Jane possessed at least one more attribute that hadn't made Turner King's list. It was something she'd confided to him in her letters. She was nursing a broken heart, which intrigued him more than it should have for one simple reason — he'd never been able to resist a challenge. Apparently, she'd been affianced to some fellow who'd died in the war. Her exact words were that part of her heart had died with him.

Or so she thought.

He had every intention of reviving her heart. She just didn't know it yet.

The train whooshed into the station with a blast of whistles and a screech of brakes. Onlookers clapped, cheered, and waved to friends and loved ones through the windows.

Keegan's heart thumped with anticipation and a healthy amount of fear. What if Eliza Jane didn't like what she saw when she met him? What if she'd been hoping for someone more educated or talented like her and her friends? Or someone richer, perhaps, who could restore the life she'd been accustomed to while growing up?

He glanced down at his denim trousers, wondering if he should've dressed up a little more. Or taken another bath this morning to wash off any dust he'd missed the night before.

While his mind swam with misgivings, the train ground to a halt and the doors to the cars rolled open. Bodies gushed onto the platform. Most of them were men. A few of them were families with children. Many were engulfed in the embraces of loved ones. A few folks were driven away in the wagons and coaches.

Keegan craned his neck over the crowd, anxious to catch a glimpse of the four young brides who'd been traveling together. For what had to be the thousandth time, he thanked the good Lord that his mail-order bride had not been forced to make the trip alone.

As the crowd of travelers started to thin, his heart thumped a little harder in his chest. *Please, God, don't let them turn up missing like the ones from Savannah!* He couldn't bear the thought.

As the parade of passengers dwindled to a trickle, his patience finally snapped. No longer able to wait, he left his post at the base of the platform, jogged up the steps, and strode toward the nearest train car.

"What are you doing?" Jameson called after him.

Instead of answering, Keegan ducked inside the car. A quick glance around its interior made his heart pound even harder.

There they were!

In the rear of the car, four southern belles were straightening each other's hair, re-tying bows, and pinching color into their cheeks. Well, three of them were, anyway. The fourth one made Keegan drag in a breath of wonder.

My bride. Eliza Jane was exactly who and what she said she was. Her long, dark hair was hanging down her back, brushed to a full shine. Reading glasses were perched halfway up her pert little nose. The black dress she was wearing made her fair skin appear all the more pale.

There was a watchful air about her, too. While the other young ladies continued to primp, she appeared to be standing guard. For this reason, she was the first one to notice his presence.

Her hazel gaze latched on to his and held for a breathless moment.

"Miss Ferrell?" He advanced on her with a hand outstretched.

To his amazement, she whipped out a handgun and pointed it at his chest. "Please state your identity, sir."

"I'm your groom." He grinned down at her, delighted to no end that his lovely bride-to-be was equipped to defend herself.

Though relief flooded her eyes, she demanded primly, "I reckon you have proof of that?"

"That I do, Miss Ferrell." He produced his copy of their marriage contract, unfolded it, and held it out for her to scan.

She tucked her gun inside her reticule and silently extended a black gloved hand to him.

Folding the contract back into his pocket, he raised her hand and pressed it to his lips. "Keegan Ford, at your service." He lowered her hand and added in a huskier voice, "Today and for the rest of our lives."

His heartfelt declaration brought a faint glimmer of tears to her eyes. Unfortunately, there was no way of knowing if she was moved by the sentiment behind his words, or if she was simply saddened by the reminder that she would soon belong to him. The fact that she was still dressed in mourning after all this time told him that the ghost who held her heart had a mighty powerful grip on it.

Lassoing the affections of Miss Eliza Jane Ferrell might pose a bigger challenge than he'd originally anticipated.

"Were you notified about the dangers we encountered on our way out of town, sir?" She shot a concerned look at her friends as she spoke.

"We were." He kissed her hand again. "Be assured that any future threats will have to go through my brothers and me before they get to you."

Her wary expression relaxed. "I think I'm going to like being married to you, Mr. Ford."

He winked at her. "That's the plan, Miss Ferrell."

Though she'd not pinched her cheeks before his arrival, a rosy blush chased away her paleness.

By now, his brothers, Bo Stanley, and the marshal had entered the train car. Turner King remained in the doorway facing out, ever the vigilant lawman.

Bo, however, was standing in front of one of the southern belles — a petite blonde who was utterly dwarfed by his impressive height and breadth. His earlier nervousness was gone. At the moment, he looked nothing short of enchanted by the notion of joining hands in holy matrimony with the doll-like creature.

Carlton and Redding looked equally entranced by a pair of redheads in fetching blue dresses. They looked so much alike that Keegan wondered if they were twins.

"No," Eliza Jane affirmed in a low, melodic voice, making him realize he must have asked the question aloud. "Magnolia is actually a year older than Emmaline. I can understand your confusion, though. They do look a lot alike." She quickly pointed out that Magnolia's face was a little rounder, and that Emmaline was much shyer than her sister.

Keegan wasn't sure that either of those details would be

enough for him to tell them apart. He nodded, though, knowing she was only trying to be helpful. Picking up her black travel bag, he crooked an arm at her, inviting her to take it.

She wordlessly curled her hand around his elbow.

Something deep and elemental shifted inside his chest at her show of trust.

"I fear you were not entirely honest about one thing in your letters, Miss Ferrell," he informed her quietly as he led her from the train.

"Is that so?" Her voice held a hint of wariness as they exited the car together.

"Yes. You look nothing like a hoyden." He grinned down at her to drive the point home that he was only jesting.

A chuckle bubbled from her. "I was hoping if I lowered your expectations far enough, you wouldn't be too disappointed when you saw me."

He scowled at her. "You're so lovely that there was never any real risk of that."

"I used to be," she sighed as he led her down the steps to the pair of carriages he and his brothers had rented from the livery. Bo Stanley followed directly behind them with his tiny doll-like bride-to-be.

Keegan raised his eyebrows at his affianced. "When was the last time you looked into a mirror, Miss Ferrell?"

She blushed again. "A few years ago, before I lost my home and..." Her voice dwindled for a moment before renewing in vigor. "Believe me. It was a relief not to have to watch the rest of me fade away while my hands shriveled to nothing in a wash bucket."

He was silent as he lifted her into the carriage and took a seat beside her. Bo Stanley lifted the blonde woman in next. The two of them took a seat on the opposite bench.

He waited until they were engrossed in conversation again

before picking up where he'd left off with his own bride-to-be. Plucking her hand from his elbow, he deliberating removed her glove.

"What are you doing?" she bleated, looking distressed.

"This." He lifted her hand to his mouth again, kissing her bare fingers one by one.

They trembled a little, though she did not pull them away.

"Hard work is nothing to be ashamed of, Miss Ferrell." He helped her slide her glove back on. Then he tucked her hand around his arm once again. "I'll give you fair warning. My own hands are riddled with calluses and scars." He dipped his head to speak directly in her ear. "You'll find a few scars in a few other places, too." *Eventually.* Though he couldn't wait to enjoy the intimacies of marriage, he'd been coached by the proxy attorney representing the bridal agency that such things might take time.

"Eliza Jane," she returned softly. "That's what my friends call me. I'd like to think we'll become friends."

"I'm Keegan. Just Keegan." He turned his head to gaze deeply into her eyes, silently assuring her that he intended for them to become more than friends — much more.

She shyly held his gaze, searching his features as the carriage lurched into motion. Jameson was driving the team outside. The two youngest Ford brothers, Chevy and Lance, were driving the team behind them. They'd been guarding both rigs the whole time their older brothers were meeting and collecting their brides from the train station.

Keegan boldly stared back at Eliza Jane, memorizing every classical line and angle of her delicate features. She was a truly stunning woman, one who checked every item on his wishlist and then some. He hadn't been tossing out idle compliments about her loveliness earlier just to be nice. What excited him the most, though, was the fact that she appeared to be as lovely on the inside as the outside.

"What are you thinking?" Her question held a breathless note.

"That I'm not disappointed in our bargain. Not one bit. I can't believe you ever worried about something so foolish."

Her long, dark eyelashes momentarily fluttered against her cheeks. "I'm not disappointed either, Keegan."

Her boldness captivated him all the more. "Good. That was going to be my next question."

She sniffed in disbelief. "When was the last time *you* looked in a mirror?"

He was amused by the way she hadn't hesitated to toss his words back at him. "There's one hanging over my wash basin. Why?" Speaking of his wash basin reminded him that they would be starting out in a cozy, four-room cabin together. He hoped she didn't mind, since it was all he'd had the time to build for them so far. His brothers had helped. The soonest they could probably add on to it was next spring. If it got too suffocating in the meantime, she could visit the farmhouse where Jameson and his wife lived as often as she wanted. Since she and Penelope were already friends, they'd get along famously.

"Are you really going to make me spell it out for you?" Eliza Jane demanded.

Her irritated tone made his grin widen. "Yes, please."

"You're a very handsome man, Keegan Ford." She gave him a withering look. "As if you didn't already know that!"

He guffawed, falling a little deeper beneath her spell. "I reckon your opinion on the topic is the only one that matters, since you'll be the one looking at me for the rest of your days."

She gave a delicate shudder. "Are you ready for this?"

His eyebrows rose. "To marry you?"

"Yes." Her voice dropped to a whisper.

"I'm ready."

"What made you ready?" she pressed.

"I don't know. I've never thought about it." He wasn't sure why it was such a big deal to her. "I reckon it's because I've always wanted a family of my own someday. What about you?" The moment the question left his mouth, he regretted it. It was a foolish question to ask a woman who'd lost her family, her wealth, and the man she loved.

"Do you want the truth or the sugar-coated version?" she returned in a low voice.

"The truth, Eliza Jane. Always."

"Very well. I used to dream of marrying for love. After the war, I no longer harbored such notions. At that point, I figured I would never marry at all."

"I'm sorry for your loss, Eliza Jane." He reached over to cover the hand she had resting on his arm. He'd been wanting to say that to her ever since she'd written to him about losing her beau. It seemed best to wait and say it in person, though, so she could both feel and hear his sincerity.

"Thank you," she murmured, dropping her gaze.

"I reckon the entire journey was hard on you," he added quietly. *Might as well get all the tough things out of the way right now.* "Traveling all the way to Texas to marry someone who isn't...him."

She nodded mutely and seemed to be having a hard time meeting his gaze again.

In for a penny. He plowed forward resolutely. "It is clear to me you're still grieving. Maybe a part of you will never stop grieving. All I ask is that you try to find a little room in your heart for your new family in El Vaquero. Not right now or even today. But eventually."

When she finally raised her gaze to his, it was glistening with unshed tears.

Though his heart wrenched in sympathy, he kept silent so she could say her piece.

"Something tells me that won't be too hard." Her voice was choked with emotion. "In time."

Without thinking, he reached up to cup her cheek. "I will never ask you for more than you're ready to give me." He needed her to understand that she could take their marriage at whatever pace she needed to. His mother and stepfather had taught him that the best things in life were worth waiting for.

A tear slipped down her cheek. "You are the kindest man I've ever met, second only to my father."

His gut told him that was high praise, indeed, coming from her. He used the thumb of his glove to wipe the dampness from her cheek. "I wish I could've met him."

Her smile was sad. "Though he didn't entirely approve of the first man I was engaged to, I think he would've liked you."

"Oh?" He liked the sound of that. "Why is that?"

She bit her lower lip contemplatively. "You're self-made like he was. Unlike my dearly departed beau, my father didn't inherit a cent of his fortune. He built his shipping company from the ground floor up." Pride glowed in her eyes. "One nail and railroad tie at a time."

What fortune? Keegan's eyebrows rose in puzzlement. "What happened to his company?"

Her expression grew shuttered. "The war," she supplied bleakly.

It was the kind of answer that brooked more questions. A war in itself didn't have the ability to vanquish a company or a man's fortune. There had to be more to the story. However, Keegan deemed it wiser to wait until his bride-to-be was better rested and less sad to press the topic further.

The sound of gunfire popped outside the walls of the carriage, making all four occupants straighten in alarm.

"What's going on?" The blonde woman's fine-boned features scrunched in alarm.

Bo was already sliding the leather curtain aside to thrust his head out the window.

"Don't," she begged, tugging frantically on his arm. "We have no idea who's out there."

He obligingly ducked his head back inside the window, offering her a bashful smile. "I reckon you're right, Olivia Joy."

Olivia Joy. Keegan was glad to finally have a name to put with the petite woman's face. It suited her kind temperament.

A bullet smashed into the windowsill, returning his attention to the commotion taking place outside the carriage. The path the bullet had taken to embed itself in the wood would've gone straight through Reverend Bo Stanley if he hadn't been so quick to follow the urging of his affianced. As their team of horses screamed in alarm and broke into a run, Bo used his hulking shoulders to shield her much smaller frame as he dragged her to the floor of the carriage.

Keegan did the same with Eliza Jane. "Stay down," he commanded in a low, terse voice as he and Bo reached for the pistols in their holsters.

More shots were fired at the carriage, making the horses run faster.

"I saw two men on horseback following us," Bo growled to Keegan. "Guns a-blazing with black scarves tied over the lower part of their faces."

A chase ensued, during which Keegan and Bo took turns firing at the outlaws from the windows of the carriage.

"Turn over the women, and we'll let you go," one of the outlaws hollered.

Over my dead body! Keegan gritted his teeth, estimating they were less than a mile from the outer perimeter of Ford Ranch. Their range riders would surely hear the gunfire and come to their aid soon.

Bo raised himself to his knees and fired another shot out

the window. Then he sank back to the floor, clutching his shoulder.

"You've been hit," Olivia Joy cried, reaching for him.

"Stay down," he groaned.

"I will if you will," she returned evenly. She was already easing his buckskin jacket from his shoulder to examine his injury. "Thank the good Lord. The bullet only grazed you. Fortunately, I brought a roll of bandages with me." She reached for her travel bag.

Bo watched in bemusement as she fussed over him. "Never fear, darlin'. I'm still in good enough shape to marry you."

She rolled her eyes at him as she unearthed her roll of bandages, along with a tiny flask of liquid. She quickly swabbed away the blood on his shoulder. "I wasn't planning on letting you off the hook, reverend."

His wide, humor-filled eyes caressed her. "You're going to make a fine minster's wife.

"So long as I keep you alive until we reach the church," she muttered darkly.

He guffawed, reaching for her hand to give her fingers a noisy kiss. "A very fine wife," he repeated, sounding utterly besotted.

Keegan clenched his jaw as he eyed the approaching foothills. *Any time now. Any time now.*

It felt like hours before a bevy of range riders erupted like lava in the distance. They spilled down the sides of the knoll, parting to make room for the two carriages to pass between them. His shoulders sagged with relief at the volley of gunfire they aimed at the bandits.

Help had finally arrived.

Chapter 3: Heiress Woes

ELIZA JANE

Before Eliza Jane could catch her breath, the shoot-out was over. The pair of carriages bearing the four brides-to-be and their prospective grooms skidded to a halt.

The drivers leaped to the ground, shouting back and forth. "You alright back there?" her driver called. From something she'd overheard Keegan say to Reverend Stanley, he was the oldest Ford brother, Jameson. He certainly sounded like an older brother the way he was taking charge and performing an accountability check.

"We're fine," the drivers of the other carriage shouted back — two more Ford brothers, if she had to venture a guess. They had the same Hispanic good looks as Jameson and Keegan, albeit a younger, cockier version.

Keegan assisted her off the floor and back onto the bench so she could straighten her clothing and collect her scattered emotions. "Are you hurt?" he asked anxiously, reaching for his Stetson, which had been knocked off. He set it back on his dark, wavy hair.

"I'm fine, thanks to you." He and Bo had gallantly shielded their brides with their bodies.

"I'm glad you're unhurt. In case you're wondering, we made it to the church." He pointed out the window, smiling wryly.

She nodded, finger-combing her dark hair from her face and removing her reading glasses. She was fortunate they'd not fallen off and shattered during the harrowing encounter with the outlaws.

She tucked them safely inside her reticule before scooting closer to the window for her first glimpse of the church. It was a one-story white adobe building with a steeple. "I'm sorry for the trouble we seem to have brought with us." She'd been so hoping they'd left it behind in Atlanta.

Keegan's expression didn't change. "It's not the first time we've been waylaid by highway robbers, but they were no match for our range riders. They never are." His voice was infused with pride.

She wasn't questioning the skills of his staff, and he knew it. In his own way, he was simply trying to reassure her.

However, she had no intention of pretending what had just happened was anything less than a second attempted kidnapping. "You heard their demands. They wanted you to turn us over to them."

"Well, we weren't the least bit tempted to give in to the rogues." He reached out to lightly run a gloved finger down her cheek. "The moment you agreed to marry me, you secured the protection of everyone who lives and works at Ford Ranch."

He wasn't simply bragging. She could tell he meant every word he said, which increased his appeal to her all the more. She longed to lean into his strength and rest her head against his shoulder.

He was even handsomer than she'd pictured while reading his letters. He was also better off financially than he'd let on. His denim trousers and boots looked new, and his suit jacket was impeccably tailored. In return, he was about to join hands with a dusty, impoverished southern belle in a wrinkled mourning dress.

"I'm still sorry for all the trouble trailing our heels." She shook her head regretfully at him. "I would understand if you're having second thoughts about marrying me." She wouldn't blame him if he returned her to the train station, dropped her off, and left without looking back.

He snorted. "You clearly have no idea what kind of man you're marrying, but you will soon enough." His dark eyes glinted with a dozen unspoken promises.

She felt her cheeks heat beneath his admiring gaze. "Surely, you have to be wondering why those men are pursuing us."

"I intend to do a lot more than wonder." His gaze grew steely.

"I honestly don't know what they want from us." She silently pleaded with him to believe her. "I truly wish I did."

"I have a few ideas." His voice was grim.

"You do?" Her eyes widened in surprise.

"It's a theory I'm still working on." He pushed open the stagecoach door, leaped to the ground, and reached back inside for her. "If it's all the same to you, I'd rather focus on getting married right now. We can meet with the marshal afterward about this outlaw business."

"You truly still want to marry me?" She scanned his features anxiously as he lowered her feet to the ground.

"Someday we're going to laugh about this conversation when we repeat it to our grandchildren, Eliza Jane." The glint of humor in his dark eyes made her heart give an unexpected little flutter.

He glanced over the top of her head and called to his friend, who was still inside the carriage with Olivia Joy. "Quit your blubbering, Bo, and get out here. It's only a scratch."

The minister's broad shoulders appeared in the doorway.

He had to shift his body sideways to fit through it.

Eliza Jane scanned his face curiously as his large boots thudded to the ground. She wondered why he looked like he was about to laugh. She had her answer when he chortled to Keegan before spinning around to assist his bride-to-be, "Maybe I like being fussed over."

Keegan made a sound of derision. "Well, save some of it for later. I'd like to be wed sometime this century." Then he sobered. "That way I can get my bride safely back to Ford Ranch. I suggest you do the same, reverend." He cast a look in the direction the outlaws had ridden off in. "I'm not liking the idea of y'all being alone out here at the church this evening." Or tonight. Or in the coming days, for that matter.

"We have a visiting minister," Bo reminded. He'd called in a pastoral friend of his to perform his wedding ceremony to Olivia Joy today. "With a little urging, he might be convinced to stay the night."

"One night won't be enough. You may stay at the farm-house with our blessing." Jameson strode up to them, frowning at the makeshift bandage on Bo Stanley's arm. "I thought you said everyone in your carriage was alright!" He pinned his brother with an accusing look.

Keegan rolled his eyes. "Don't start in. He's been coddled enough already by his lovely bride-to-be."

Olivia Joy gave a tinkling laugh as her Paul Bunyan sized groom lifted her to the ground like she weighed no more than a baby chick. "Someone has to tend to the reverend. Heaven knows he's not going to get much sympathy from the rest of you brutes." Her twinkling blue gaze softened the insult.

Bo Stanley snickered. Loudly. "Couldn't have said it better myself." His large hands lingered possessively on her tiny waist. "As you can see, I have my work cut out for me. It's no easy task ministering to such uncouth cowboys."

Keegan curled his upper lip at his friend. "Is anyone else

trying not to gag?"

Eliza Jane joined in the round of chuckles that followed, and allowed her groom-to-be to lead her into the church.

It was a little bigger on the inside than she'd pictured from the outside. The entry foyer held a row of coat hooks on either side of the door. A sanctuary stretched beyond it with two rows of rustic wooden pews. A narrow aisle ran between them. Long, rectangular windows lined the walls on both sides, and an enormous pulpit anchored the raised platform beyond the altar, probably because Bo Stanley was such a big man. A large wooden cross graced the wall behind the pulpit.

"Well?" The reverend bent to whisper something in Olivia Joy's ear that made her turn pink. Then he strode to the front of the sanctuary and jogged up the stairs of the platform. His pastoral friend from El Gato was awaiting him beside the pulpit. He was an aging man with a head of white hair and an equally snowy beard. Though it wasn't Sunday, he was in his Sunday best brown plaid suit.

He stepped up to Bo with a hand outstretched, but Bo ignored his hand and clapped him a bear hug. After conferring together quietly for a moment, the elderly minister stepped to the side of the platform and folded his hands, waiting.

Bo took his place behind the pulpit and beckoned with both hands. "If the grooms will please step forward with their lovely brides, we'll get these weddings started."

The youngest two brothers, Chevy and Lance, sidled down to the front row and slid into the pew on the right. Jameson dashed up one of the side aisles and stepped outside. Eliza Jane hoped it didn't mean the outlaws had returned.

Keegan waggled his eyebrows playfully at her, quickly laying that fear to rest. "The rest of our family has arrived. Jameson went to fetch them." He studied her intently. "Are you ready for this?"

She tasted a moment of panic. *Am I ready for this?* Her

fingers momentarily dug into the crook of his arm. He wasn't the suave southern gentleman attorney that her first beau, Mark Hudson, had been. He didn't have anywhere near the polished mannerisms, the cultured accent, or the tailored Italian silk suits. He did, however, know how to handle a gun and fight off a pair of would-be kidnappers. He'd protected her only minutes earlier with his own life. And in the coming weeks, he would stand between her and poverty, hunger, and danger. Marrying him was truly her best chance of survival. They both knew it.

Even so, he didn't rush to elicit an answer from her. Watching the myriad of expressions play across her features, he covered her hand with his own. "Just breathe, Eliza Jane."

She nodded, dragging in a shuddery breath. Her vision blurred as her thoughts flew back to her family. If only her mother was still alive to give her a few last-minute tidbits of advice. If only her father could walk her down the aisle. If only she had something to wear besides the funereal black dress she had on. If only...

The door to the church opened and closed behind them. "My dearest friends," Annabelle Vasquez breathed. "Oh, darling," she trilled to the man at her side, "we made it in time!" Her melodic voice surrounded Eliza Jane like a soothing balm, assuring her that everything would be alright now that her closest childhood friends were together again.

She glanced over her shoulder, surveying the expectant young mother with drenched eyes. Annabelle looked so happy on the arm of her range rider husband, Ethan. She gave an excited little wave of welcome to those gathered at the altar, then made a shooing motion to urge her husband forward. As he guided her into a pew, his beaming gaze never left her and her swollen belly.

Penelope was standing right behind them, clutching one of Jameson's arms. On his other arm was a tiny Hispanic woman in a white blouse and cape over a brightly embroidered skirt. She had to be his mother.

The door opened and closed again, and a middle-aged man with frost at his temples stepped inside and hurried to catch up to their group. "This is all of us." He waved a hand apologetically to Bo Stanley. "Our apologies for the delay."

"Let us begin." The reverend shot a questioning look at Keegan and Eliza Jane. They were the only couple who hadn't finished making their way to the front of the sanctuary. Even Olivia Joy was standing to one side of it, looking expectantly up at him.

"I'm ready now," Eliza Jane whispered to Keegan.

He squeezed her fingers and escorted her to the front of the church. His brothers stepped aside and made room for the two of them to take the center spot in front of the altar.

"Friends and family," Bo Stanley drawled with a long, searing glance at his own bride-to-be, "though the trip home was a bit harrowing, every mile of it was worth the unions we are about to celebrate."

Keegan leaned closer to Eliza Jane to rasp, "He's still milking that little scratch on his arm."

She gave a muffled expulsion of laughter. Then she froze in consternation at the realization they were being irreverent in the House of God. Tightening her fingers on Keegan's arm, she hissed, "Behave!"

Bo Stanley gave them a knowing look that made her feel like he could see right through her. She flushed uncomfortably and tried to focus on what he was saying. He was quoting an age-old passage about love from the Book of 1 Corinthians in the Bible.

"Love is patient, love is kind," he droned. "It does not envy, it does not boast, it is not proud. It does not dishonor others, it is not self-seeking..."

Keegan kept his head bent next to Eliza Jane's head,

adding small commentary here and there. "Except in the reverend's case, when he wants a little extra sympathy from his special lady."

Another bubble of silent laughter whooshed out of Eliza Jane. She tried to cover it with a cough.

Bo Stanley watched them with bemusement. "It is not easily angered, it keeps no record of wrongs. Love does not delight in evil but rejoices with the truth."

Keegan muttered, "And occasionally stretches the truth to impress a certain lovely—"

Eliza Jane squeezed his arm as hard as she could to shush him.

"It always protects," Bo sounded like he was finally winding down, "always trusts, always hopes, always perseveres." Then he said a brief prayer and launched into their exchange of vows.

"Keegan Ford," he boomed a little louder than she thought was necessary. "Do you take this woman to be your wife, to have and to hold from this day forward, for better, for worse, for richer, for poorer, in sickness and in health, to love and to cherish, until death do you part?"

Eliza Jane was fascinated that such a large, bushy bear of a man could say such a lengthy mouthful without stumbling over a single word.

"I do." Keegan's voice was clear and resolute. He straightened at her side, keeping her arm curled around his.

"Miss Eliza Jane Ferrell." Reverend Stanley's voice dropped a few degrees in volume as he repeated the beautiful vow to her.

"I do." She drew a deep, shaky breath, hoping Keegan was convinced that she meant it. She'd never been one to give her word lightly. No matter how many more days, months, or years of grieving lay in store for her, she would honor her wedding vows for the rest of her life.

"You may seal your union with a holy kiss," Bo Stanley concluded with the faintest hint of a smirk.

A kiss? Good gracious! Eliza Jane barely had time to suck in another breath before Keegan's gloved hand tipped her chin up. His head descended over hers, and his hard mouth seamed against her lips. And immediately grew gentle.

It was only the second time in her adult life that she'd been kissed. Mark Hudson had punctuated their engagement with the quickest peck on the lips. His mouth had felt cold and a little clammy, probably because he was so nervous.

Keegan Ford's mouth, however, moved over hers with unhurried confidence. Despite the winter temperature outside, his lips were warm and possessive, tender and cherishing. His touch echoed his sentiments from earlier that he was a man who was very much ready to be married. There was a thinly concealed longing in him that she sensed he was fighting to suppress — like a horseman keeping a tight grip on the reins of a spirited stallion.

The kiss ended as abruptly as it had begun. "My bride." Keegan's dark eyes burned into hers, both seeking and claiming at the same time.

All she could do was summon a tremulous smile in return. There were no words to describe the emotions he'd stirred in her. By the end of their kiss, she could think of nothing and no one but him.

My husband. A feeling of wonder stole over her at the knowledge that he'd made her forget — at least for a few seconds — the heartache she'd carried around for so long. She studied the strong line of his jaw and traced his square chin with her eyes, wondering what it was about him that she found so mesmerizing. According to his letters, he possessed no college degrees. He wasn't well traveled, nor was he well versed in many topics other than ranching.

Though his brothers were standing on either side of them,

it sounded like they were reciting their vows to Magnolia and Emmaline from a great distance.

Only when the aging minister from El Gato moved to stand behind the pulpit did Eliza Jane return her attention to the platform.

Nodding respectfully at Bo Stanley, he waited until the younger reverend left the platform to go stand by Olivia Joy at the altar. Then he repeated the same wedding vows to the fourth and final couple waiting to be wed.

Eliza Jane had missed most of Magnolia and Emmaline's part of the ceremony, but she was very much aware of the way Bo kissed Olivia Joy afterward. He swept her entirely off her feet and swung her in a full circle while his mouth was sealed against hers.

Her face was glowing like a summer rose by the time he set her back on her feet. Only then did Eliza Jane realize he'd not once so much as winced from the effort it took to use his injured arm.

"See what I mean?" Keegan drawled in her ear. "He was never in much pain. He was just carrying on and on to get her sympathy earlier."

"Apparently, it worked." She chuckled softly, not the least bit disappointed to see her friend so happy. In the past, Olivia Joy had been the quietest one in their circle of friends, more inclined to disappear into a book than carry on a conversation. Or fall beneath the magic of her latest burst of inspiration when she was painting.

Eliza Jane's heart squeezed at the memory of how long it had been since her friend had been able to enjoy the luxury of such pastimes. For the past few years, all six of them had worked without ceasing, scraping together every penny they could to pay their rent and keep food on the table. There'd been no extra coin for ribbons or books, hobbies or sweets.

The moment the wedding ceremony ended, the petite

Hispanic woman rushed up to Keegan and Eliza Jane, her brightly embroidered skirts swishing around her ankles. "I'm so happy for you, son!" She kissed him on the cheek, then reached for Eliza Jane's shoulders. "I am Paloma Ford Clanton, his mother." The scent of rose water enveloped them.

"Pleased to meet you, ma'am." Eliza Jane's smile felt a little shaky as she endured the woman's close perusal. She wished all over again that she'd worn something besides black on her wedding day. Her time of mourning had long since ended. Poverty was the real reason she remained in the same faded dress, day after day.

"You may call me Paloma, my dear." Paloma lightly pressed their cheeks together. "What a joy it is to have another son happily wed! You are an answer to his prayers and mine."

"I think you meant to say you are overjoyed to have three more sons wed," Carlton corrected in a jovial voice. He stepped closer to enclose his mother in a bear hug.

"That I do." She hugged him back, her dark eyes growing misty with affection. "Four sons married. Only two more to go," she sighed with a laughing glance at her two youngest sons. "When the time is right, of course. They're still so young."

Eliza Jane followed the woman's gaze. "How old are they?"

"Eighteen and twenty." She grimaced. "Some would say twenty is plenty old enough to be wed, but neither of them are ready. All in God's timing." Her gaze was infused with motherly concern. "They'll know when that is, just like the others did."

Annabelle and Penelope converged on their friends next. The six women formed a tight huddle punctuated by a thousand sighs and happy tears. They embraced and chatted a mile per minute to catch up on everything they'd missed in each other's lives.

Paloma finally burst into their midst. "How about we take

our celebrating back to the ranch?" Her smile was welcoming. "Annabelle and Penelope have helped me prepare a feast worthy of a quadruple wedding!"

In minutes, Eliza Jane found herself back in the carriage with the bullet embedded in the window opening. She shivered at the sight of it.

"Cold?" Without waiting for an answer, Keegan unbuttoned his suit jacket and draped it around her shoulders.

"You'll freeze," she protested, trying to wriggle out of it and hand it back.

"Nah, I have you to keep me warm." He boldly curled an arm around her and tugged her against his side. "My lips are a little cold, come to think of it." He nuzzled the soft skin of her earlobe, eliciting a breathy chuckle from her.

"Liar!" His lips didn't feel the least bit cold. They seared a warm trail everywhere they touched.

He gave an unholy snicker. "If the reverend can get away with stretching the truth about—"

"I heard that," Bo Stanley interrupted. He was seated across from them again, with one large arm slung loosely around Olivia Joy's shoulders. She had her left hand splayed out in front of them, gazing in amazement at the new ring she was wearing.

Eliza Jane could only surmise her husband had given it to her. It was a swirl of gold vines that looked as delicate as the slender finger it encased. A red ruby winked from the center of it like a winter rose.

"Oh, that reminds me!" Keegan reached inside one of the pockets of the suit jacket he'd placed around her shoulders. He drew out a small black box and flipped open the lid. A radiant square diamond rested there in a simple white gold setting. "It's yours. I hope you like it."

Eliza Jane couldn't immediately find her voice.

"Please assure me you like it," he repeated a tad anxiously.

"Oh, but I do!" Her voice sounded oddly breathless to her own ears. "You got this for me?" She couldn't believe her rugged cowboy had purchased something so beautiful and so costly. How had he been able to afford something so valuable?

He lifted the ring out of the box and slid it on her finger. "From the moment I read your first letter, I wanted to do something special for you. On paper, you were everything I'd ever dreamed of."

"And now that we've met?" Her voice was barely above a whisper.

"You are more than that." He placed her hand bearing his ring over his heart.

"Here and I thought I was nothing but trouble," she murmured shakily, trying to bring a note of levity back into their conversation.

"All women are trouble, or so I've heard." He winked at her. As he leaned closer to brush his mouth against her fore-head, his thumb lightly grazed her lower lip, reminding her of the way he'd kissed her to seal their vows. "I'm leaving our next kiss up to you." He spoke against her temple. "I meant what I said earlier about not asking for anything you aren't ready to give."

Flushing, she met his gaze. "Are you asking me to initiate the next kiss?"

"More or less." His voice dropped to a caressing note. "Or at least let me know when you're ready for me to kiss you again."

"I will." She blushed harder.

They rode past a cabin with a canyon view, then pressed upward into the foothills. It didn't take long before the land leveled out again into a wide, flat mesa.

Ford Ranch was sprawled in the distance, surrounded by a bevy of outbuildings and a new looking three-story barn. They drove up to it without any further brushes with danger, though they did spy a pack of wolves just beyond the tree line.

The story-and-a-half adobe home had a festive pine wreath hanging on the front door. A red velvet ribbon was tied at the top center of it. Inside the farmhouse, a dark green fir tree rose all the way to the ceiling. It was decorated with berries strung together with thread and more red velvet ribbons. Beneath the tree, a pile of gifts were wrapped in brown burlap and tied with twine. Small sprigs of pine and berries were tucked into the twine.

They were soon seated in the dining room at long wooden benches on either side of the rustic farm table. The entire party at the church was there, plus one additional guest, a U.S. Marshal named Turner King.

He'd arrived in a black top hat and somber black overcoat, both of which were now hanging on the hall tree. His gold badge glinted like a warning over his heart, reminding everyone present that there was more at stake today than a wedding celebration.

He waited until everyone was finished eating before leaning his forearms on the table and grimacing at them. "I know your wedding day isn't the best time to bring this up, but—"

"I think I know why that brothel is after our brides," Keegan interrupted coolly. He reached for Eliza Jane's hand.

"By all means." Turner King gestured for him to continue.

"My wife mentioned something earlier about her father being a self-made man. She went on to say that he made his fortune in shipping." He glanced down at her. "Those were your exact words, were they not?"

She nodded sadly.

"It's the same old song we keep hearing from our lovely southern belles," he continued in a tight voice. "They moved in the highest circles of society until the war stripped them of everyone they loved and everything they owned. All six of them."

Eliza Jane wondered where he was going with his speech.

"Or so they thought." He waved at Annabelle. "As it turned out, an unscrupulous set of individuals tried to hide the fact she was the true heiress to a railroad spur. Next, Penelope turned out to be the real heiress of Copeland Plantation. It makes me wonder if the outlaws bent on carting off the rest of our brides are after the same thing — their inheritances." He nodded at the marshal to yield the floor back to him.

Turner King's expression was hard. "Your theory has merit, Keegan. Money always attracts criminals." He moved his shrewd gaze to Eliza Jane. "Do you know the circumstances surrounding the loss of your family's fortune?"

"Unfortunately." She glanced at Magnolia, Emmaline, and Olivia Joy, silently asking their permission to share what she knew.

"His name is Cane Fraser," Olivia supplied bitterly. "Go ahead and tell them about the scoundrel."

Eliza Jane's mouth tightened. "He's the man of business who served the Ferrel, Dixon, and Banks families before the war began. He claims our assets dwindled to nothing while our menfolk were away fighting. When they failed to return, he pitched us from our homes one by one."

Turner King eyed them soberly. "So, let me get this straight. Eliza Jane, your family owned a shipping company."

She nodded mutely.

"And ours owned an opera house that was packed every night," Magnolia confided in a regretful voice.

"My father was a painter," Olivia Joy declared bitterly. "His gallery attracted art enthusiasts from all over the continent."

Mr. King pointed at Eliza Jane. "A shipping company," he repeated.

She nodded again.

He pointed at Magnolia and Emmaline next. "An opera house."

They wagged their heads.

"And an exclusive art gallery." He pointed in Olivia Joy's direction last, looking like he was pondering something. "Are they still in business?" he inquired abruptly.

Olivia Joy spread her hands. "We had no way of knowing. We spent every waking moment the last few years trying to survive."

Magnolia brushed a red curl back from her cheek. "We took in mending and washing, barely managing to keep our rent paid and food on the table."

Her sister grimaced. "We were exhausted and hungry. Sometimes, folks forgot to pay us or refused to pay us. Not once during that time did we have the opportunity to pay a visit to the opera house."

Keegan laid his hands on the table, palms flat. "Are you thinking what I'm thinking?"

The marshal snorted. "I reckon we're all thinking the same thing."

"We're not out of danger yet, are we?" Eliza Jane felt sick to her stomach.

"Not quite." Her husband reached for her hand and threaded his fingers through hers. "Something tells me that all three of your family firms are still open for business. It's the only reason I can fathom that four impoverished southern belles would continue to pose such a threat to anyone."

Turner King's expression was impossible to read. "Obviously, Cane Fraser bears looking into. I'll widen my investigation immediately."

He said his goodbyes and took his leave of them.

Chapter 4: Tied Down

KEEGAN

Keegan was reluctant to part with his new bride for even a few minutes, but his mother had other ideas.

"Go visit some more!" she ordered briskly, shooing her hands at the younger women to get them moving. "Not only is it your wedding day, you have a lot of catching up to do. Gray and the boys will help me clear the table." She smiled fondly at her new husband. They were newlyweds, themselves, having only exchanged their vows a month ago. Their relationship, however, went back nearly a decade. That's when he'd left a profitable livery to handle the horses at Ford Ranch. After the death of Paloma's first husband, he'd become a permanent fixture in her life and the lives of her sons.

Keegan remained at the dining room table, following his bride's willowy frame with his gaze as she stood and moved to the living room with her friends. It was his greatest hope that the two of them would someday share what his mother had found with Gray. Keegan was enormously grateful for the senior cowboy's mentoring throughout his latter teen years. Without Gray's unfailing wisdom, there was no telling what kind of men he and his brothers might've become. They owed their faith, work ethic, and best decisions to him. And now they had the honor of calling him their father.

The moment Gray stood with his plate in hand, the Ford brothers shot to their feet and starting clearing dishes from the table. Bo followed suit. The plates, silverware, and cups were washed in record time, and the leftover food was covered and stored for later.

After the last plate was dried and stacked in the cabinet, Paloma left the kitchen to join the other womenfolk, while the men took a seat around the table again.

Keegan caught his oldest brother's eye. "Besides increasing our patrols, what do you suggest?" There'd been dangers surrounding the arrival of the first two mail-order brides into their midst. The Fords had learned a thing or two along the way about dealing with thugs.

The side door to the kitchen opened, and a stomping sound ensued as the newest arrival kicked the snow from his boots. Moments later, Ethan Vasquez entered the room, rubbing his hands from the wintery weather conditions during this morning's patrol.

Keegan was glad their lead range rider had arrived in time to take part in their discussion. He'd been the first in their ranks to wed a mail-order bride. Now that he and Annabelle had a child on the way, he was especially anxious to batten down the hatches in terms of security.

From the knowing look he and Jameson exchanged as he took his seat, Keegan suspected he'd overheard his question about what they should do next. Both men looked like they were fighting an inner battle. That meant they knew something they hadn't yet shared with the rest of the group.

While Gray disappeared into the kitchen to grab the plate of leftovers Paloma had set aside for Ethan, Keegan pinned him with a scowl. "What aren't you telling the rest of us?" It irked him to realize Ethan and Jameson had been keeping secrets. Once upon a time, there'd been no secrets between him and his oldest brother.

Ethan shrugged, sending a helpless look in Jameson's direction. "It's not my place to squeal."

"Fine. Jameson can do it." Keegan shot his brother a warning look.

Jameson waved a hand at Ethan. "Technically, he's the one who discovered it. Gray probably knows more about it than both of us combined, though."

Keegan swiveled his head to his stepfather as he re-entered the room bearing Ethan's lunch. "You're in on it, too?" *Am I the only one who doesn't know what's going on here?*

"Only by marriage," the middle-aged man responded with a twinkle in his eyes as he set the plate in front of their lead range rider. He left the room again and returned with a tall mug of coffee.

Keegan huffed out a frustrated breath and his stepfather reclaimed his seat at the head of the table. "We could play guessing games all afternoon, or we can get back to doing our jobs and protecting what's ours." *Isn't that what this meeting was supposed to be about?*

At Jameson's and Ethan's pleading looks, Gray threw his hands into the air. "You do realize my wife is going to scald my backside for telling you this?"

"Oh, for crying out loud!" Keegan fisted his hands on the table. "Somebody, spill the beans. I don't care who gets scalded in the process, so long as the rest of us know what we need to do to keep our wives safe."

"It's a good thing you're sitting down, since this is probably going to come as a shock to the rest of you." Gray shook his head, looking rueful. "Your mother owns and operates The Western Moon Agency."

Keegan sat riveted for the space of several heartbeats. Then he snorted. "P. Claiborne." He repeated the name of the agency owner out loud, finally understanding why it had always sounded familiar. "I should've known the P stood for Paloma." And Claiborne was her maiden name recorded in their family Bible. He should've put two and two together and come to this conclusion long before this morning.

"Why would Ma go and do a thing like that?" Carlton ran a hand through his dark hair, standing it on end.

It was pretty obvious to Keegan. "To have a say in our choice of wives, of course! Not that I'm complaining." He was more than content with the mail-order bride he'd been matched with. Their mother knew all six of her sons better than they knew themselves. He knew without asking that she'd done what she did out of nothing less than the utmost concern for their happiness.

"No complaints from me, either."

"Or me."

"Or me."

Once they got over their initial surprise, the other married men around the table didn't look the least bit perturbed by Gray's revelation.

"Back to your earlier question, though." Between mouthfuls of food, Ethan sat forward on the bench to address Keegan. "I'll make sure we maintain round-the-clock patrols on our perimeter. Now might also be the right time to move forward with our plans to make El Vaquero a self-sufficient community."

Jameson wagged a finger at him. "Agreed. The sooner we can reduce our dependence on the goods and services in El Gato, the better. Every time we travel to and from there, we're exposed. Highway robberies and ambushes have doubled in the past year."

For convenience sake alone, Keegan very much liked the idea of not having to ride several miles to send every blasted telegram. But Jameson was right. Becoming a self-sufficient community would greatly increase their security. "I know Ethan's working the angles with the railroad to get a spur going out this way." That would be a real game changer when that happened. Keegan didn't bother asking him for an update, because Ethan shared every detail the moment it became available.

Instead, he steered the conversation back to things within their immediate control. "Plus, we staked out our future Main Street months ago. We've got space set aside for a bank, post office, feed mill, livery, blacksmith, land office, and a few shops."

"The livery could initially double as the stage office," Gray mused, drumming his fingers on the table. "With my background, I could easily help out with both until they get off the ground."

"Speaking of doubling things up, the church can house the school until we're ready to give 'em their own building," Bo Stanley offered magnanimously.

Keegan shot him a mocking grin. "Annabelle is the only one in the family way so far. I think we have a few years before we need to worry about that."

"Maybe. Maybe not." The reverend shrugged. "Some of the homesteaders we recruit might bring their families. Either way, it never hurts to plan ahead."

Keegan smirked, not quite ready to quit teasing his friend. "If that scratch on your arm isn't paining you too much, you could help us dig another well out that way. We're going to need it once Main Street gets built up."

"Aw! Are you still jealous of all the attention I got today?" Bo winked at him. "Bet you're wishing you're the one who got winged by a bullet, so your bride could tend and bandage you."

It was so true that Keegan nearly started to guffaw, but he didn't want to give Bo the satisfaction. "Seeing as how soft and breakable you are," he countered loftily, "it might make sense to move another one of us closer to Main Street soon." He curled his upper lip at the man. "Don't need you getting winged too often." Bo was a little more exposed than the rest of them since he lived the farthest from Ford Ranch. It was one thing for a mountain man to live alone in a church parsonage. It was another thing entirely to have a new wife join him there, especially one being targeted by outlaws.

"What do you have in mind, cowboy?" Bo drawled.

"A boarding house, if you're referring to Keegan and me." Eliza Jane sailed back into the dining room and slid backwards onto the bench beside her husband. She leaned her elbows on the edge of the table, giving him a challenging look.

He waggled his eyebrows at her. "Exactly how long have you been eavesdropping on our conversation, Mrs. Ford?"

"You were bellowing to wake the dead," she informed him with a haughty tilt to her high-born nose. "It's not eavesdropping if folks are talking so loud that there's nowhere to escape the noise."

"Noise, eh? Is that all you think of our manly planning session in here?" He would've loved to hook an arm around her slender waist right then and there to see what kind of lovely noises he could elicit from her if he kissed her. A squeal of surprise? A sigh of pleasure?

She ignored his question and asked one of her own. "I honestly wouldn't mind living closer to Olivia Joy if you're serious about moving someone closer to the church."

He studied her for a moment, tickled to no end by the sincerity he read in her gaze. "We'd have to vacate the four-room castle I built for us."

She didn't bat an eyelash. "Oh, you'd be building us a much bigger place, Mr. Ford, if we relocate to Main Street."

"How big?" He knew he was staring, but he couldn't seem to tear his gaze away from her. The way her dark hair tumbled like a waterfall past her shoulders made his fingers itch to reach out and touch it. She was so beautiful that it made his chest ache. He couldn't wait to see her in something besides mourning clothes.

She made a soft humming sound in the back of her throat as she considered his words. "A boarding house should be two stories, I think. We'd need a kitchen, dining room, living room, and parlor on the first floor. Plus a private apartment in the back for you and me. That would allow for...hmm." She paused and appeared to be doing a mental calculation. "Six rooms on the second floor. Maybe eight, depending on their size."

"I'll help cook the meals for our guests." Paloma's voice wafted over them from the doorway. "If Gray is going to be downtown helping out with the livery, I may as well do my part."

There was no way Keegan was saying no to that. "If you're cooking, Ma, we'll have no trouble recruiting more folks to move to El Vaquero." It was time to start selling and leasing land to other homesteaders. The Fords and their key staff members had been chewing on the details for the better part of a year. They were ready.

As he continued to study his new wife, it dawned on him that her presence in his life was largely what was making him feel ready. They were going to make a good team. He could feel it in his bones.

"Is that your way of telling me yes?" she taunted.

His gaze briefly dropped to her too-thin frame and faded gown. "It would be a lot of work getting started. Are you sure this is something you want to jump into so soon?" She'd only recently been extricated from a life of drudgery in the city.

"I'm no stranger to hard work," she protested. She waved a hand vaguely in the direction of the living room where most of her friends were still sitting. "None of us are."

"I am well aware, but my question still stands. Are you sure this is what you want?"

"I know what you're thinking, and I appreciate your concern." Her voice was infused with gratitude. "But we didn't travel all the way to Texas expecting to be endlessly pampered and indulged—" She broke off her words when he started grinning.

A breathy chuckle escaped her. "I know I said in one of my letters that I wanted to be treated like a princess, but I was mostly jesting."

"Mostly?" He was thoroughly enjoying the twin spots of pink their exchange had brought to her cheeks. The princess topic was one he fully intended to take up with her again once they were alone.

She brushed away his teasing with a wave of her hand. "This is different from what happened to us in Atlanta, because this time we had a choice." She clasped her hands beneath her chin as she swiveled to face him on the bench. "We traveled west for a fresh start, and we fully intend to contribute to the new life we're building together here."

"You'll need help," he informed her flatly. "No way am I going to allow my wife to do all the mending, cleaning, washing, bookkeeping, and everything else required to run a whole blasted boarding house. I'll help you every chance I get, but running the ranch will continue to require long hours, too."

"Like Paloma, I'm happy to help," Olivia Joy's voice wafted shyly over them. She stepped into the room and moved behind Bo to rest a hand on his shoulder. "Since we won't need the school up and running right away, I'm going to need something to do." She glanced down at her husband, clearly hoping for his input. "I'm in the best position to pitch in, considering we'll only be living a few doors down."

Bo reached for her hand and used it to tug her down onto the bench beside him. "I don't have any objections, Mrs. Stanley. Like Keegan, I just don't want my woman slaving away from dawn until dusk. Someone," his voice grew teasing, "has to come home and tend to the reverend now and then."

"There you go again." Keegan shook his head at his friend.

"I was only agreeing with you," Bo pointed out in a scoffing voice.

"Then what are we waiting for?" Jameson jumped back into the conversation with alacrity. "I know it's cold out this time of year, but the fields are fallow. Other than herding and range riding, we've got fewer demands on our time between now and spring thaw than we'll have the rest of the year."

Gray nodded and added his two cents to the mix. "Any prospective homesteaders we bring through will like the sight of new construction. It'll show them we mean business about the next phase of growing this town."

"The new boarding house will additionally give them a place to stay while they build," Eliza Jane pointed out.

"I like how you think." Keegan nodded in admiration at her. Clearly, his bride had a good head on her shoulders. It made him angry all over again that her late father's man of business had more than likely swindled her out of her family's fortune. Though he harbored no hopes of getting it back, he genuinely hoped the marshal's investigation turned up something against Cane Fraser that would lead to his arrest. Men like him didn't deserve to remain at large, conning innocent women out of every last dime they had to their names.

Carlton and Redding stood in unison.

"We'll grab the axes," Carlton drawled.

"Time to start chopping down trees," his younger brother added.

FOR THE NEXT TWO WEEKS, ELIZA JANE DIDN'T SEE much of Keegan. He rose from the couch in their cozy little cabin at first light, left for work, and didn't return home until after dark. Because of the two attempted kidnappings, he insisted she remain behind at the ranch, well within the safe perimeter of the range patrols.

At first, she'd enjoyed piddling around their cabin, but she'd quickly grown bored. No, she didn't miss her back-breaking schedule in Atlanta, but she needed more projects to fill her time. The only upside to being bored was that her hands were getting a much-needed break from the soap suds. Thanks to a jar of handmade lotion Annabelle had gifted her, her hands were beginning to look like they belonged to a real lady again. The scratches and calluses were quickly disappearing, and her fingernails had grown out enough to be trimmed and filed smooth.

Penelope had given her a set of work gloves to protect her newly restored skin, for which she was enormously grateful. She wore them every time she dusted and cleaned the cabin, which she'd done from top to bottom several times over already. There wasn't a speck of dust left anywhere, but she had nothing better to do.

She cleaned the windows inside and out until they gleamed. She mended a small tear in the living room curtains. She visited each of her friends and helped them out where she could — sewing baby clothes for Annabelle and assisting in one of Penelope's many quilting projects. She always arrived early to dinner at the ranch so she could help cook and set the table. She even collected pine cones and sprigs of winter berries in the woods and used them to decorate the mantle in her cabin.

The Monday before Christmas dawned frosty and cold. As usual, Keegan was already gone for the day. Eliza Jane rolled out of bed quickly, but her movements slowed as she dressed.

She wondered how in tarnation she was going to spend yet another day alone. There was, quite literally, nothing left for her to do at the cabin. Her pantry was stocked to overflowing with canning jars and jams that she'd made under Paloma's careful instruction. They'd also made candles, soaps, and a variety of medicinal remedies during the last two weeks.

When a few snowflakes fluttered past the window in the living room, she finally decided she was done huddling inside the safety of the cabin. She'd either talk one of the range riders into taking her to the construction site of the new boarding house, or she'd walk there herself.

She banked the fire in the hearth. Then she bundled up in her hooded cloak, gloves, and scarf. Tying on her ankle boots, she stepped onto the front porch to find out how cold it was. A breeze was whistling down the mountains. It whipped at her hair and cloak, making her shiver.

Good gracious! It felt even chillier this morning than the day before. Logic told her she wouldn't make it far on foot in this weather. Not without another layer, at least. Or two. Or three. Trying and failing to quell another shiver, she longingly thought back to the days when she'd owned more clothing than a body could shake a stick at.

While growing up, her wardrobe had been overflowing with riding habits, cloaks, and gowns for every occasion — cold weather, warm weather, and everything in between. Wondering what had become of her belongings, she wished she'd had the foresight to change out of her black mourning gown before being pitched into the street.

Little had she realized she'd still be wearing the same black gown a few years later. It had been mended dozens of times, and the color was starting to fade from so many washings. Unfortunately, she had nothing to replace it — not even a bolt of fabric to start sewing a new gown. Money had been too tight.

Until now.

Keegan had urged her more than once to place an order that he and his brothers could fill for her at the General Store in El Gato. Though he'd not precisely asked her to replace her dress, he kept insisting she buy "whatever she needed." He nearly always ended that statement by giving her gown a pointed once-over.

She'd been reluctant to spend his money, though. He'd already done so much for her — giving her a roof over her head, a warm place to sleep, and plenty of food. They'd only been married for two weeks, during which he'd stayed busy at the construction site. Wouldn't his funds be better spent on paint and nails right now? And what about all the items it would take to furnish the place for their future boarding house guests?

Purchasing a new dress felt frivolous and unnecessary in light of everything else they had going on. With a gusty sigh, she ducked her head against the wind and trudged in the direction of the farmhouse where Penelope and Jameson lived. Maybe she could talk her friend into lending her an extra cloak or scarf without precisely stating why she needed it.

Or not.

Her heart sank at the sight of Paloma making her way to the house from the other direction. Like a watchdog, her mother-in-law kept an eye on everybody and everything at Ford Ranch. Beneath her watchful gaze, it would be a lot harder to slip away unnoticed to the construction site on Main Street — not impossible, though.

"Good morning!" Paloma caught sight of her and fluttered a cheerful wave in her direction.

"Good morning!" Eliza Jane waved back. Their paths converged on the front veranda.

Penelope must have been watching them through the window, because she opened the door before they could

64

knock. "Come in and share the fire." She excitedly ushered them inside. "I have a pot of tea warming and biscuits about to come out of the oven. I was going to send them to our menfolk on Main Street, but I made plenty. There's enough for us, as well."

"What do you have planned for today, dear?" Paloma shot Eliza Jane a curious look as they removed their gloves and cloaks and hung them on the hall tree. They strolled together toward the dining room.

"Nothing, I'm afraid." Eliza Jane's voice was wry. "My husband is away, our cabin is cleaner than clean, and I am fresh out of projects." Paloma had been nothing but kind to her. There was no point in being less than honest. After a quick mental debate, she decided to speak her mind. "What I wouldn't give to pay a visit to the boarding house today!"

"Me, too." Paloma's smile was warm with sympathy. "Gray says they've just about got it framed out."

"Keegan said the same," Eliza Jane sighed. "But it's not the same as seeing it for myself." Another thought struck her. "Has Gray been insisting you stay home, as well?"

"Yes." Paloma chuckled, not looking nearly as disturbed about that fact as Eliza Jane was. "Our safety is their top concern these days, my dear."

"I know, but—"

Paloma waved a hand to cut off her protest. "I know it's frustrating, but they couldn't bear it if anything happened to a single one of us."

"I'm not completely helpless, you know." Eliza Jane gave her a petulant look. "I personally thwarted a thief. A few minutes later, my friends and I escaped a fire and outran a set of kidnappers."

"And the next time they pursued you on horseback with no less than four guns firing in your direction," Paloma reminded softly. "Nobody is bullet proof, my dear. Not even big, strapping Bo Stanley." It was a sobering reminder that one man had already sustained an injury while defending them.

Eliza Jane nodded glumly, knowing she was right. "I can't live with my head under a pillow for the rest of my life, either. Keegan can't expect me to. There are risks every time I wake up and every time I step out of the house." It was the cost of being alive, wasn't it?

"There won't be nearly as many risks after the marshal gets to the bottom of this Cane Fraser business," Paloma retorted in a firm voice. "And he will. Mark my words. Until then, he made my sons promise to keep a close eye on their brides. He believes there's a serious and imminent threat to your collective safety."

Eliza Jane's ears perked at her mother-in-law's choice of words. "Did he track down that new brothel, then?"

"Not yet, but he says he has a good idea where it's located."

"Oh, really?"

"Yes. That's why I was walking so quickly to get here. I figured you ladies would appreciate the update."

By now, Eliza Jane was hanging on her every word.

"He came by this morning to tell Gray he took a low-level cattle rustler into custody. During the interrogation, the fellow made some reference to a brothel buried in the mountains west of El Gato. When Turner tried to question him further, he started pitching a fit. Begged him to either forget what he'd said or shoot him on the spot."

Eliza Jane stared at her mother-in-law in fascination. "It sounds like his reference to the brothel was a slip of the tongue."

"For sure. He was scared out of his skin that someone might be able to trace the leak back to him."

"Did the marshal determine what the cattle rustler's, er... connection was to the brothel?" Eliza Jane's face turned red with embarrassment, since she could think of only one reason why an outlaw would visit a place of ill repute.

"He refused to say, but Turner is inclined to believe he was merely...ahem...a patron of their services. Not the owner of the operation."

Eliza Jane's stomach pitched sickeningly as her mother-in-law verified her worst fears. She was suddenly not as anxious to override her husband's request for her to remain at the ranch where it was safe. Better to be bored than deflowered.

Paloma watched her from the corner of her eye as she held out her hands to warm them by the fire. "If you'd like, you could help me with a sewing project today."

Eliza Jane swallowed an inward groan. She was sick to death of washing and mending. She had to fight to keep the sigh out of her voice as she inquired, "What do you have in mind, ma'am?"

"A new gown for one of my dearest daughters-in-law," she returned cheerfully. "The only bride in El Vaquero who hasn't sewn the first stitch on her new wardrobe."

Eliza Jane's eyes widened at the realization that the woman was speaking about her. "Is that so?" She inwardly scrambled for a way to change the subject.

"You know it is. The question is *why*?"

Eliza Jane grimaced. "I've no wish to waste funds on something so frivolous."

"I think we both know that Keegan doesn't see it that way," Paloma chided gently. "I know for a fact he has a tidy amount of savings in the bank, and he's never been anything less than generous with those he cares about."

There lay the sticking point. Eliza Jane turned her face away. "We've barely had time to get to know each other, certainly not long enough to inspire those kinds of feelings."

"You're his wife, Eliza Jane. He wants to provide for you."

"He's done more than enough for me already, ma'am."

"More than you feel you deserve, I suspect. What with your heart still belonging to another and all?"

Eliza Jane caught her breath sharply, wishing her mother-in-law wasn't quite so astute. "You don't miss much, do you?"

"Not where my sons are concerned, no." Paloma didn't sound the least apologetic about that fact. "They mean everything to me, which means you mean a great deal to me, as well."

Eliza Jane's head whipped in her mother-in-law's direction. "I've done nothing to—"

"You pledged your life and loyalty to him," the woman interrupted doggedly. "You've made his sparse little cabin a home. You've cooked and mended for him. You're kind to him. You seem to understand his dry sense of humor better than a lot of folks, and I dare say you're growing a mite fond of him."

"Of course, I'm fond of him," Eliza Jane exploded. "He's a wonderful man!" Keegan was hardworking and honest. He was good to her.

"On that, we agree." His mother smiled in appreciation. "Once you are through with your mourning," she gestured at Eliza Jane's gown, "I think it would make him happy to see you in some color."

"What if I'm never finished mourning?" It wasn't just the loss of her beau that grieved her. She'd lost her mother to an illness, her father and brother to war, and her home to creditors.

"You're young. You'll heal in time," Paloma assured softly. "If it's any comfort, Gray and I have been praying nonstop about those things since your arrival."

"Thank you," Eliza Jane choked. "In all honesty, I'm sick to death of this dress. But there isn't a shade of fabric on the continent that will restore what I've lost. The war took everything from me, Paloma. Everything!" she repeated fiercely.

Paloma was silent for a moment. When she started speaking again, her voice was hushed with empathy. "I'm sure Job in the Bible felt much the same way, my dear, but God restored him." She reached over to touch her hand. "Just like He's going to restore you. It's alright if you don't believe it right now. I have enough faith for both of us."

The woman's kindness made Eliza Jane's shoulders shake with silent sobs. "What if I can't love again?" she quavered. "What if I can't ever be the kind of wife Keegan deserves?" Her many fears and misgivings came tumbling out like a flood. As wonderful as her new life in Texas was, maybe she didn't deserve one drop of it. "Maybe you should have matched your son with someone else. Have you considered that?"

"No." There was no hesitation in Paloma's answer. "I made my decision about the two of you on my knees, my dear. And after our conversation this morning, I'm more convinced than ever that you are exactly the right bride for my second son." She patted Eliza Jane's arm before taking a step back. "So, whenever you're ready to start sewing on that new gown together..."

Eliza Jane dabbed at the edges of her streaming eyes with both hands. "Like I said," she gulped, "I have absolutely no other plans for today."

"You do now!" With a girlish squeal of excitement, Paloma turned and threw her arms around her. "Things will get better from here. I promise."

"I know," Eliza Jane murmured damply against her mother-in-law's shoulder. "They already are. I reckon that's why I feel so guilty."

"Guilty!" Paloma drew back in astonishment. "You have nothing to feel guilty about. Of all people, I should know." She scowled in concern at Eliza Jane's damp face. "When I lost my first husband, I didn't think I would ever love again, either. Then Gray came along." She gave a tinkling laugh. "He was like a gift from Heaven. He stepped in and helped out with my boys, mentoring and loving them like they were his own. My heart never stood a chance against such selflessness."

"How did you know you were in love again?" Eliza Jane couldn't fathom walking down that path a second time. A person's heart could only bear so much

"When my sons started throwing their hat into the ring for mail-order brides, I suppose." Paloma sounded rueful. "They were arm twisting all the fellows around here into joining them in their grand new adventure — Ethan, Bo, and even Gray." She shook her head at the memory. "At that time, nobody knew I was the one doing all the matchmaking behind the scenes. The mere thought of having to match Gray Clanton to a mail-order bride nearly crushed my soul. That's when I realized that I'd gone and fallen for him myself."

"You mean it happened without you even knowing it?" An airy expulsion of disbelief eased out of her.

"It usually does." Paloma hugged her again before lowering her arms to her sides.

"I think I would know it was happening," Eliza Jane whispered. Keegan was so direct, so intense, so achingly good looking, and an incredible kisser, to boot. Her face burned at the memory. He wasn't the kind to grow slowly on another person like moss.

"I think you will, too, my dear," Paloma assured with a secretive smile, like she knew something that Eliza Jane didn't. "I believe that with all of my heart."

Chapter 5: New Construction

KEEGAN

Three days later

Keegan's shoulder blades prickled with foreboding. Someone was watching him and his brothers while they worked. Bo was swinging a hammer right alongside them, as usual. From the day he'd arrived in El Vaquero, he'd taken part in every major project and most of the smaller ones, too. Though it was Christmas Eve, they'd voted unanimously to keep working at least half a day longer on the boarding house project before taking a holiday break.

Keegan took a step back from the last piece of wood he'd hammered into place, liking the fact that they were nearly finished with the framing. He was especially excited that the coming snowstorm had held off long enough for them to mount and hammer the V-shaped roof trusses into place. They were putting the finishing touches on a few window and door openings this morning and expected to be done with that by noon. The day after Christmas, they'd begin placing shingles and adding the outer walls.

Now that the framework was only a few nails shy from

being completed, he could easily picture the floor plan that Eliza Jane had envisioned. He could just as easily picture her willowy figure bustling through the rooms, bringing her special brand of energy to the place. He could tell by the way she plied him with questions every chance she got that she was anxious to receive her first in-person tour.

As risky as it was to bring her out here right now, he was going to find a way. Soon.

He reluctantly pulled his gaze away from the frame to do a quick but thorough survey of the surrounding foothills. The prickling sensation between his shoulder blades intensified, affirming that they were indeed being watched.

"What's wrong?" Bo glanced across the building from the door frame he was working on.

"My gut says there's someone out there." It gave him a sick feeling in the pit of his stomach. The last time a set of thugs had trolled through Ford Ranch, they'd burned down their biggest barn. It had really set them back. Fortunately, Gray Clanton had pitched in some of his savings to rebuild it, insisting he believed in their community enough to invest in it. He was a full partner now that he'd married their mother.

Bo nodded grimly, running a shirtsleeve across his glistening brow. "As much as I hate to say this, maybe we shouldn't all go on holiday at the same time, after all. The range riders can't patrol every inch of the perimeter around the clock, and we can't afford to sustain any more vandalism."

Keegan was thinking the same thing. Ethan Vasquez already had their team of cowboys working day and night in a constantly changing rotation to make their schedule impossible for passers-by to predict. They couldn't possibly ask one thing more of the expectant father.

"I'll take the first shift," he offered quickly. "Y'all go on and enjoy your Christmas Eve." It wasn't as if he and Eliza Jane had anything going on in the way of intimacy. As much as he was hoping and praying to change that between them in the future, he was starting to worry they might never enjoy a real marriage. A full two-and-a-half weeks had passed since their wedding day, and she'd made no attempt to repeat their kiss. Maybe he shouldn't have left their second kiss entirely up to her, since it might never happen now.

It was a depressing thought.

A lunch bell clanged in the distance. Ever since they'd commenced construction on the boarding house, Paloma Clanton had been clanging her bell louder than ever to signal their meal times.

Jameson held up a fist to call a halt to their work. "Ma's gonna pitch a fit when you don't show up for lunch," he warned.

"She'll understand." Keegan was sure of it. What he was less sure of was if his new bride would miss his absence. For all he knew, she'd be relieved not to have to spend Christmas Eve with a fellow who wasn't the one she continued to mourn for.

Bo sidled up to him while his brothers were loading tools and supplies back into their work wagon. "I'd like you to look me in the eye and tell me your offer to serve first shift isn't about something other than pure benevolence."

Keegan glanced away, knowing he couldn't do that. "Leave it alone, Bo."

"If we were simply friends, I would, but I'm also your pastor."

"Then pray for me." Keegan slapped his hands against a set of studs to test their stability. It wasn't necessary, since every inch of the frame was stable. However, it gave him something to do besides look at his best friend.

"I do. Every day. And for Eliza Jane, too."

"Don't stop." Keegan's gaze flickered briefly to the hulking mountain man. "Seems to me your marriage to Olivia Joy is already running on rainbows and rose petals." He knew he probably sounded bitter and envious, but he couldn't help it.

"She says she likes being a minister's wife." Bo's expression softened. "That makes her one in a million in my book. A lot of women wouldn't have been interested in joining hands with a fellow bent on walking the straight and narrow."

Keegan was happy that his friend was so compatible with his new bride. "Eliza Jane says she's always been the quietest one in their bunch, but she talks up a storm when she's with you."

Bo spread his hands, grinning. "What can I say? Most men of the cloth are easy to talk to. It's in our job description." His smile faded a few degrees. "But it's not all rainbows and rose petals, as you say. Like a garden, every relationship requires a certain amount of cultivating."

Keegan snorted. "At least, you're not competing with a blasted ghost for your wife's affections."

"Maybe not, but that didn't make her instantly fall in love with me, either. Those things take time." He bent his head closer to Keegan's. "It also takes cultivating, in case you missed that part. That means you're going to have to carve out some time to spend with her. To talk. To get to know her better. To pray together."

"We talk." Keegan jutted his chin stubbornly.

"When? In the middle of the night?" Bo shot back. "Because you're always the first to show up here and the last to leave. If I didn't know you better, I'd think you were anxious to leave home and in no hurry to return."

Keegan shook his head in warning. "Just let it go, Bo. Brow beating me like this isn't going to change anything."

"Problem is," Bo continued, as if he hadn't heard him, "if a big, dense fellow like me thinks you're avoiding your wife, chances are your wife thinks you're avoiding her, too."

Keegan clenched his jaw. "What if she doesn't want me around?" He glared at his friend. "Have you considered that?"

"You coming, Bo?" Jameson called, giving them a curious stare. The brothers had finished loading the wagon and picking up most of the construction debris. Chevy and Lance were hitching the horses.

"Nah, I'll follow in a bit." Bo waved them on ahead of him.

"Just go," Keegan groaned beneath his breath for Bo's ears alone.

"Nah, I think I'll stay a bit."

Please don't. However, there was no point in arguing. If Bo had made up his mind, he could be as bullheaded as the Fords about changing it.

"Alright then." Jameson gave the two of them another searching look. He adjusted his Stetson a little lower on his forehead. "Fire your weapons if you need us to come running."

Keegan nodded in agreement. Then he folded his arms and leaned back against the door frame to study his friend. "If I remain out here, the holiday will be that much easier on my wife. My presence constantly reminds her that I'm not the man she wishes was at her side."

Bo gave a resigned huff and leaned back against the other side of the door frame beside him. "You know what? I never pegged you for a coward."

"Insults will get you nowhere," Keegan growled, hating the truth behind the minister's words.

"You know I'm not wrong."

"I can't make my wife want me."

"Why not?" Bo demanded, swiveling his head in Keegan's direction.

Keegan shrugged. "I reckon you can't force someone to feel something they don't."

"Then make her feel something," Bo groused.

"How?" Keegan would dearly love to make Eliza Jane Ford feel something in his direction, but everything he'd tried so far had failed.

"By showing her how important she is to you and how important your marriage is to you."

"Again, how?"

"Be kind. Be patient. Be a good listener. Make her smile. Then make her laugh. Pray for her every single day. Keep her safe. Make her feel beautiful and cherished. Help her. Encourage her. Become the one person in the world she can't live without."

Keegan mulled over his friend's words, mentally checking off the items that he'd succeeded in doing already. To his despair, he came up woefully short. He wasn't sure he'd made it past the first item. Kindness. He'd been kind to her. That was it.

He lifted his Stetson to run a hand through his hair, knowing he hadn't been terribly patient with her. An absent husband wasn't much of a listener, either. And being gone as much as he had certainly didn't give a man many opportunities to make his wife smile or laugh. He'd prayed a little about their marriage, but his prayers had mostly been the self-pitying kind — begging the Lord to soften Eliza Jane's heart toward him.

"You're right," he admitted heavily, clapping his hat back on his head. "I've been avoiding her. I wanted so badly to get married. I wanted what Ethan and Jameson have found with their wives. And when it occurred to me that it might never happen to us, I reckon I started to lose heart."

Bo nodded gravely. "That brings us to our next question. Do you regret marrying her?"

"No!" Keegan was so adamant that he pushed away from

the wall. He rounded on his friend. "What kind of question is that?"

"A fair one at this point." Bo waved a hand. "In case you've forgotten, it's a mail-order marriage, my friend. There are provisions in your contract that allow you to dissolve your union during the trial period, should either of you find it unsatisfactory to continue."

"I don't care what our contract says! I would never annul our marriage!" Keegan stared at him like he was crazy. He viewed marriage as was one of those once-in-a-lifetime things, and he wasn't looking for a way out. "If she wants to dissolve our union, I reckon there's nothing I can do to stop her, but I won't be the one to do it." It was discouraging to be reminded about that part of their contract. He'd all but forgotten it.

"The annulment option only remains on the table so long as you haven't, er...consummated things yet."

"Good gravy!" Keegan nearly choked on his tongue. *We just established the fact that I've been avoiding my wife.* "What do you think?"

"I think you're sleeping on the couch," Bo retorted without humor. "I'm married to your wife's best friend, remember?"

"Then why are you fishing for information if you know so much about my blasted marriage?" Keegan snarled. It was bad enough to be married to a woman who didn't love him and probably never would. It was even worse finding out she'd been filling the ears of others about their problems.

He stomped around the clearing before facing his friend again. "What else has my wife said about me to your wife?"

"Not much."

"That doesn't sound like nothing."

"Fine. She feels guilty about spending your money on herself."

"Why?" Keegan threw his hands into the air. "I know

money is tight, but I'm not a pauper. I can afford to provide for her."

"It's not that." Bo made a face and seemed to be searching for the right words. "She doesn't feel she has the right to a single penny of it while she remains in mourning. She doesn't think it's fair to you."

"That makes no sense." Keegan shook his head, thoroughly perplexed. "I knew she was in mourning when I married her. She was honest about everything in her letters to me." Brutally so and laughingly so. It had been so much easier to write to her from a long distance than it had been to converse with her now that they were living together.

"There's an idea." Bo wagged a finger excitedly at him.

"I'm not following you." Keegan was only half listening. He was too engrossed in the memory of how sassy and humorous his wife had sounded in her letters. He rather missed writing to her.

"You should write her another letter."

"What?" Keegan curled his upper lip at his friend. "And stick it in the mail?"

"You could. If I was you, though, I'd just hand it to her afterward or leave it some place she'd be sure to find it. If you write her a nice enough letter, she might even write you back."

Hope stirred in Keegan's chest. He'd read her letters so many times, they were becoming dog-eared and ragged. "I'll say this. It's not the worst idea you've ever come up with."

"In that case, I'll bring you a pen and some paper. You can write her a Christmas Eve letter, and I'll carry it with me to lunch." Whistling, Bo reached for his hammer, propped it against his shoulder, and marched determinedly toward the church.

Keegan stared after him, not knowing whether to laugh or throw something at him. He finally settled for gathering his thoughts about what he was going to write to his wife. While he waited for his friend to return, he climbed to the roof of the boarding house for a better view of the distant mountains.

Making his way to the top peak, he straddled it like it was a horse. Shading his eyes against the sun, he searched for any sign of life out there. According to the latest fellow Turner King had arrested, the elusive new brothel he kept hearing about was more than a rumor. It lay west of where he was currently sitting. He'd never before heard of anyone opening a secret brothel in the mountains. Places like that were usually built in more populated areas near saloons and such.

Darkness breeds darkness. It had been like that since the beginning of time.

Then again, if the owners of the brothel were filling it with hostages instead of bonafide employees, it made sense that they'd want to hide them from the public eye. Anger curdled in Keegan's chest at the thought of women being held there against their will. The possibility that they were being targeted for their fortunes and family names felt doubly unfair. Turner King really needed to get to the bottom of this case, and soon.

Bo Stanley's large figure trudged back in Keegan's direction only a minute or two after he disappeared inside the church building. In his hands were the promised writing materials. He snickered as he caught sight of Keegan on the roof. "You've got the best view in the house." Glancing in the direction Keegan was staring, he quickly added, "Any signs of trouble out there?"

"Not yet." Keegan's gut told him it was only a matter of time. It was cold. Whoever was squatting in the mountains would eventually start a fire. And when he did, they'd have his location.

Swinging down from the rafters, he balanced his weight for a moment over a door frame. Then he jumped to the ground. He reached for the piece of paper Bo was holding out to him. "This is going to take a few minutes."

Bo shrugged. "Take all the time you need." His stomach growled loudly, giving lie to his words. "Just not an entire treatise, please."

Pretty sure there weren't enough words in his vocabulary to pen something that long, Keegan balanced the paper against a windowsill and reached for the ink bottle Bo was holding out to him. "Promise me you won't read it on the way to lunch."

"I promise."

"It's for Eliza Jane's eyes alone," he added in a hard voice.

"Understood."

"If she decides to read it to your wife, plug your ears."

"Oh, for pity's sake!" Bo gestured at him to continue. "Get on with it!"

Keegan started to write. At first, it felt a little awkward penning a letter to the woman he lived with, but he soon fell into the rhythm of it and simply told her what was on his heart. It didn't take nearly as long as he feared. When he was finished, he capped the bottle of ink and reread what he'd written.

Dearest Eliza Jane,

Please forgive my absence this afternoon. I had the feeling all morning we were being watched, so we're posting a guard at the boarding house.

In case you're wondering, I volunteered for the first shift. Why? Because I figured it would be easier for you to get through Christmas Eve without the constant reminder that you're married to me instead of the fellow you lost.

I'm sorry for everything you've suffered. I reckon the holidays are especially difficult. Just know that I'm praying for you and for us.

I probably shouldn't say this, but I had a talk with Bo today. Well, it was more like he gave me a tongue lashing, but we're friends so he's allowed to do that. He said you told Olivia Joy you feel guilty about spending money on yourself. Please stop feeling guilty. I knew you were grieving when I married you. That doesn't make you any less worthy of being my wife.

The truth is I'm living for the day I get to see you wear something besides black, but only when you're ready.

Yours,

Keegan

He waved the letter in the air to dry the ink. In the end, he decided it would be best not to fold it. Bo had given him his word he wouldn't read it, and Bo's word was good.

"Here." He handed the letter to his friend.

Bo made a huffing sound. "I thought I told you not to write a treatise."

"I wrote what needed to be written." Keegan's voice was dry. "Are you going to deliver it, or stand here browbeating me for the rest of the day?"

"Tempting, but no." Bo reached for the letter. "I'm too hungry." He glanced up at the sky. "I should probably ride my horse. That way I can bring some grub back to you before the storm hits."

Keegan waved him on. "Take your time. When I volunteered for first shift, I didn't expect a bunch of personal deliveries."

"Well, too bad. That's what friends are for." Bo slapped him on the back, then took off at a jog.

Keegan fondly watched his retreating shoulders, swinging buckskin fringe and all. There was just something about the mountain man that he'd always liked and trusted. The Fords were fortunate to have him for their pastor. He'd not once steered them wrong.

A ROUSING CHEER WENT UP IN THE DINING ROOM AT Bo Stanley's late arrival. Eliza Jane was disappointed to note that he was alone. She'd been hoping for a holiday surprise — maybe one of the range riders offering to take her husband's place at the boarding house or something. It didn't look like she was going to get her wish.

She ducked her head over her plate, pushing her slice of roasted wild turkey around it with her fork. It was time for her to admit the truth, at least to herself. Keegan Ford was avoiding her.

Bo walked the long way around the table, pausing briefly behind where she was sitting on the bench. She was startled when his long arm reached around her to hold out a slip of paper.

Her gaze widened in surprise. It was a piece of stationery. Someone had written her a letter!

Her heart sped as she recognized the handwriting. Snatching it from the minister, she glanced over her shoulder to send him a grateful smile. It felt a little wobbly.

"If you'll excuse me, please." Without making eye contact with anyone, she silently slid off her end of the bench and left the table.

Moving to the parlor across from the dining room, she took a seat behind the pianoforte in the corner. Though the narrow bench wasn't nearly as comfortable as the sofa, it was the only place in the room where she would be out of everyone else's line of sight.

Only after she was seated did she lift her husband's letter with a shaky hand to read what he'd written. Once she was a few sentences into it, his words blurred on the page.

Oh, my lands!

She had to blink to clear her vision and continue reading. When she finished the letter, she pressed a hand to her rapidly beating heart. It was such a kind gesture for him to have written her like this. He sounded so raw and honest, too. So genuine and caring. So hopeful of a better tomorrow.

His words both buoyed her spirits and filled her with despair. It underscored all over again that she'd married a good man, one she still wasn't convinced she was worthy of.

The last line he'd written was particularly special. ...*I'm living for the day I get to see you wear something besides black...* In his own, countrified, plainspoken way, he'd made her feel special. And beautiful. And married.

She fingered the skirt of the emerald green gown she and Paloma had managed to sew together in record time. It was from a bolt of cloth that her mother-in-law claimed she'd purchased on a whim and wasn't quite sure what to do with.

The high-necked winter gown they'd created from it was one of the loveliest Eliza Jane had ever worn. The delicate pearlized buttons running down her throat had been painstakingly removed from an old necklace of Paloma's that she insisted she'd never wear again. The delicate jewels added a richness to the design that rivaled all the gowns from Venice and Paris that Eliza Jane had once owned. Given the choice, she much preferred the one she was wearing right now. Maybe it was because she'd been in mourning for so long. Or maybe it was because she was married to a man who'd just written her a letter, bluntly stating he'd like to see her in such a color.

She couldn't wait to witness his reaction to it. She and Paloma had purposefully kept their sewing project a secret from everyone else, hoping to surprise Keegan with it on Christmas Eve.

A flurry of movement out in the hallway interrupted her reverie. It was Bo, tugging on his fringed coat preparing to depart. A lunch basket was resting at his feet by the door.

Eliza Jane knew without asking that he was carrying the meal to her husband. She leaped to her feet so quickly that she nearly overturned the bench she was sitting on.

"Bo?"

He spun in her direction, quirking one bushy reddish-brown eyebrow at her. "There you are! I wondered where you'd taken off to."

She fluttered Keegan's letter self-consciously at him. "If you have a few minutes to spare, I'd like to send a reply to my husband."

"I have as many minutes as you need." He looked pleased by her words.

She moved to the antique writing desk on the opposite wall, knowing Penelope wouldn't mind if she borrowed a piece of paper and a pen. Since Keegan had to be famished by now, she kept her letter short.

Dearest Keegan,

Merry Christmas Eve! Thank you for your letter and honesty. I was afraid you'd been avoiding me, and it sounds as if you have. However, I have no choice but to forgive you, since your reasons are both kind and honorable. They are also unnecessary. With how much you've been gone lately, I've grown bored and lonely — to the point of pestering everyone else in sight.

If you're receiving complaints to that end, please recall I warned you in a previous letter that you were marrying a complete hoyden. One who's been planning a holiday surprise for you. No matter how late the hour, I will remain awake until your return this evening so I can finally share it with you.

Yours,

Eliza Jane

Chapter 6: Cowboy Falling

KEEGAN

After Keegan read the letter from Eliza Jane, the hours seemed to drag. Jameson had promised to take second shift at nightfall, but each passing hour felt longer than the last. By the time the sun dipped on the horizon and the shadows started to deepen, Keegan was nearly ready to jump out of his skin from the anticipation of returning home to his bride.

He passed the final minutes of his vigil thinking about every version of her name and every possible way of pairing it with his own.

Mrs. Ford
Eliza Jane Ford
Mrs. Eliza Jane Ford
Mrs. Keegan Ford
Keegan and Eliza Jane
Keegan and Eliza Jane Ford
Mr. and Mrs. Keegan and Eliza Jane Ford

He very much liked the fact that she was a Ford now. A Ford who was wearing the diamond ring he'd purchased for her. A woman who'd stated outright in her letter that she wished her husband would stop avoiding her. A bride who didn't sound the least interested in annulling their marriage.

The sound of approaching hoofbeats made him tense. They were coming from the direction of Ford Ranch, which was a good sign. However, his shoulders didn't relax until his oldest brother rode into view on his black Mustang, Spirit.

A pair of range riders fanned out behind him.

Keegan scowled, wondering why Jameson hadn't come alone. He quickly climbed down from the rafters where he'd been perched and waited for his brother to skid his horse to a halt in front of the boarding house.

"We saw smoke on one of the ranges." Jameson pushed back his Stetson to peer at the distant mountains.

"Did you send anyone to go investigate?" Keegan craned in the direction his brother was looking.

"No. It could be a trap, and the darkness would give them the advantage. Ethan is going to keep an eye on the situation overnight. Since Turner King is stopping by for a Christmas meal tomorrow, we should probably turn the whole situation over to him and be done with it."

"Would you like me to stay out here with you tonight?" Keegan hated the thought of disappointing Eliza Jane again, but she would find it in her big, beautiful heart to forgive him. Eventually.

"No. You've been out here all day. You need your rest. Otherwise, you'll be of no use to us tomorrow."

Relief coursed through him at his brother's words, though he tried to hide it. "I don't mind heading back so long as you're keeping the range riders with you." He angled his head at the two ranch hands who'd ridden with him. They were slowly circling the construction site.

"They will." Jameson swung down from Spirit and handed the reins to him. "Plus, Bo is spending the night in the parsonage, which will give us one more man within spitting distance."

Keegan frowned in concern. "Please assure me he didn't bring Olivia Joy with him."

"He didn't." Jameson expelled a heavy breath. "She put up a bit of a fuss about it, but he held firm. Ma and Gray have offered to keep her in their guest room as long as it takes for us to secure Main Street."

Keegan gave his brother a short up and down nod as he mounted his horse. "How soon would you like us to spread the word about the lots we have for sale and rent?"

"As soon as the boarding house is complete." Jameson gave a decided nod. "Eliza Jane was right about that."

"So another couple of weeks."

Jameson tipped his head back to gaze up at the second story. "I'm liking our odds of making it happen before the end of January."

"That would be good." Keegan's heart thumped at the prospect of moving to Main Street that soon with Eliza Jane. Before he headed home for the night, he repeated his brother's words from earlier. "Fire your gun if you need us to come running."

"You know I will." Jameson tipped his hat at him.

"Goodnight." Keegan lifted Spirit's reins and dug in his heels. Though he smelled smoke on the way back to his cabin, it was impossible to tell if it was from the squatters in the mountains or the fires roaring in the many hearths at Ford Ranch. It was possible he was smelling both.

He rode Spirit to the horse barn, removed his saddle, and brushed him down. Then he jogged the rest of the way home. Since Eliza Jane had promised to wait up for him, he didn't waste time on any unnecessary detours. If anyone had important news to share, they knew where to find him.

The glow of a candle burning in the living room window

made his heart thump a little faster. Not wanting to startle his wife, he made plenty of noise, stomping up the porch stairs to announce his arrival. As he reached for the door handle, it swung open.

And there she was.

Though an icy wind was whistling across the mesa, he paused in the doorway to simply gaze at her. Though she'd not yet dipped into the money he kept in their roll-top desk, she was wearing a new gown. Her brown hair, which she normally wore down, had been swept into an elegant up-do. It was held in place by a pair of pearlized combs that matched the buttons on her gown.

Green, if he wasn't mistaken. It was a little difficult to tell the exact shade of the fabric beneath the light of the moon.

"Well, come in!" Eliza Jane urged, beckoning with both hands for him to come inside.

He had to force his boots to start moving again. "You're so beautiful." He crossed the threshold and kicked the door shut behind them. Though he longed to take her in his arms, he held back since he'd given her his word that the next move was up to her.

"Thank you." Her voice was shy. "I drew you a bath in the kitchen. Your timing is perfect, so the water is still warm."

He smirked. "Is that your way of telling me I stink, Mrs. Ford?"

Though her lips quirked with humor, she merely gave an offhand shrug. "If it is, Mr. Ford, it's your fault for marrying someone with the manners of a hoyden."

"If I may point out, I've not once complained about that fact." He followed her into the kitchen, absorbing all the changes she'd made to their cozy cabin. There was a pair of quilted placemats resting on the trestle table for two against the wall. A small sprig of pine with winter berries rose from a rosebud vase in the center of the table. The scent of fresh-baked bread clung to the room from earlier. In the short time she'd lived in their rustic little cabin, she'd managed to transform it into a place that felt like home.

"Then you're a better person than me," she tossed merrily over one delicate shoulder. "I would be brimming with complaints about me if I were in your shoes."

"Name one," he taunted, fascinated by her sudden burst of boldness. She sounded exactly like the woman in her letters — full of humor and sass. He decided on the spot that he would never get enough of this version of her.

"For one thing, I haven't kissed you since our wedding day."

Keegan couldn't believe his ears. It took him an extra moment to clamp his gaping jaws shut. "Believe me, I know." Despite his effort to match her playful tone, his voice grew a tad hoarse with longing. To tamp down on it, he lounged in the doorway, waiting to hear what she would say next.

She bit her lower lip as she spun to face him, waving a hand toward the high-back chair she'd scooted across the room beside the tub. A towel and clean change of clothing were draped across it. "It really wasn't fair of you to put the burden of our second kiss on my shoulders. Given your current work schedule, it's been a virtually impossible task."

"I'm sorry." He was inwardly kicking himself from one end of Ford Ranch to the other end for avoiding her the way he'd done. "Truly sorry." He'd been wrong to do it, and Bo was as right as rain to point it out. So right that he'd have to thank his friend the next time he saw him.

"You should be sorry, Mr. Ford." Eliza Jane slapped her hands down on her hips. "You had me wondering if it was your way of saying you did not wish to receive another kiss from me." Her voice grew shy.

"No!" He protested loudly, pushing away from the doorway. "I mean yes. I do want that. Very much."

A breathless giggle escaped her as she watched his determined advance. She waited until he was a few steps away from her. Then she pointed at the tub. An inviting fire was leaping in the hearth beside it.

It was way too bad he was so filthy. "I'll join you in the living room in three seconds," he rasped, reaching for the buttons of his shirt.

She giggled as she swept past him. "I'd like you to be a little cleaner than that," she murmured.

He turned his head her way, closing his eyes and breathing in her scent as she left the room. The little minx was wearing rosewater, probably to torment him further while he waited for her to deliver their next kiss.

In the end, he took a little longer bathing than three seconds. However, it couldn't have been much more than three minutes. He toweled off and donned a fresh change of clothing in record time. In his haste to return to Eliza Jane's side, he only half tucked in his shirt. He banked the fire in the kitchen, then made a beeline for the living room, reveling in the warmth of the fire she already had leaping in the fireplace. She'd truly thought of everything this evening when it came to his comfort.

She was perched on one end of the sofa with the full skirt of her new green dress arrayed prettily around her.

He took a knee in front of her, adoring her with his eyes.

She sat there in silence for a moment, simply gazing back at him. "It's nice to have you home, Keegan."

"It's good to be home." Wonder flooded him at the realization that she truly wanted him there. "I was a fool to stay away. I don't know what I was thinking."

Her eyes were fathomless brown pools, swimming with too many emotions to name. "I think it's because this has been as hard on you as it has been on me."

He continued to hold her gaze, enjoying her nearness

though not quite sure what she wanted him to say — what she *needed* for him to say.

"The first time you laid eyes on me was our wedding day, the same as me," she continued in the same soft voice. "After all the letters and wondering, it was a jolt to your senses, wasn't it?" She made a face. "To finally put a face to my name?"

Relief filled him at the realization that this was a topic he could safely address. "You were a lot prettier than I was expecting."

"Is that so?" She sounded surprised, which he found delightful. Apparently, there wasn't a vain bone in her body.

He reached for her hand. "In my defense, I was expecting a hoyden."

Her delighted laughter burst over him, drenching him with warmth and joy. "At least you were warned."

"You tried." His voice grew husky. "There was no way for you to truly prepare me for this."

"Are you disappointed?" she asked suddenly, her expression growing anxious.

"Not even a little." He laced his fingers through hers.

"Oh." The stricken expression turned puzzled. "In that case, there's one more thing I should probably clear the air about."

He raised her fingers to his mouth. At the last second, he remembered that their next kiss was supposed to be entirely up to her. He settled for pressing her hand against his cheek. "I'm listening."

"While you've been away, I've enjoyed some long talks with your mother. She has been very honest about how much she loved your father." She glanced away from him for a moment and seemed to be trying to collect her emotions.

As he watched her gaze grow glassy, his heart twisted. He wondered if she was thinking of her first love again.

She started speaking again in a rush. "But there's no denying how much she loves Gray now. Everyone can see how perfect they are for each other." She drew a shallow breath. "It gives me hope that maybe you and I can find...something together." She gave him a shaky smile.

He was deeply touched by the comparison she'd drawn between his mother's loss and her own. "That is my hope, too." He was thrilled to discover the possibility was still on the table. In recent days, he'd all but given up hope in that direction. "When you're ready, that is."

"We're already married, Keegan."

His heart thumped wildly at her words. "What exactly are you saying, Eliza Jane?" He sensed that the time for cross-purposes was behind them. Both of them were ready to figure out what direction their marriage needed to take next.

"I made my decision when I signed my mail-order bride contract. The day I arrived in Texas, I was ready to be married to you. You're the one who didn't seem...ready."

The breath left his chest in a huff of incredulity. "What about your mourning? I was trying to be respectful of your grief. I had no wish to rush you into anything before you were—"

"My black gown was the only gown I owned at the time," she confessed breathlessly. "If it were possible, I would've gladly worn something prettier to our wedding."

Unbelievable! His fingers tightened on her hand at the realization he'd wasted far too much time already with unnecessary worrying. Time he could've spent courting his bride and making her smile and laugh like Bo had urged him to.

"If you're truly ready to be my bride," his voice grew rough, "then kiss me."

She met him halfway, bumping noses awkwardly with him before her mouth found his.

It was sheer heaven when her lips finally pressed against his, all warm, shy, and trembly.

"Keegan," she whispered when he gently nibbled her upper lip, then her lower lip. "I've never..."

He took advantage of her breathy confession to deepen their kiss, very much liking the fact that he was the first man to kiss her like this. He intended to be the only man who ever did so.

They ended up standing by the window, clasped in each other's embrace, gazing out at the western stars together.

"Would you like to keep writing letters to each other?" She lightly trailed a finger up his arm.

"Yes." He pressed his cheek against hers. "I'd like that very much." In their letters, they'd rediscovered the magical key to communicating with each other. He never wanted to give that up again. He'd invest in a whole wagon full of paper and ink if he had to.

He was suddenly in no hurry to tell Bo Stanley just how right his advice had been. His friend would probably never stop crowing about it when he found out.

INSTEAD OF RIDING OUT AT THE CRACK OF DAWN like he had for the past two and a half weeks, Keegan escorted his bride to Jameson and Penelope's home for breakfast the next morning. It was a short walk, so they didn't bother saddling the horses.

Paloma and Penelope were hard at work in the kitchen when they arrived. The house smelled so delicious that Keegan's mouth started to water the moment he and Eliza Jane stepped through the front door. He paused in the entry foyer to help her remove her cloak and hang it on the hall tree.

Glancing around them to make sure no one was looking,

he tipped her chin up for another kiss. He had no willpower to resist the temptation when she was standing so near.

She blushed and lightly swatted his shoulder. "Someone might see us," she hissed.

"They're going to eventually find out that I'm a happily married man." He tucked a dark tendril of hair back behind one of her shell-shaped ears.

"You married a hoyden," she reminded, her dark gaze twinkling with mirth.

"A very beautiful one." He gazed deeply into her eyes. "In case I forgot to mention it, I really liked your surprise." His gaze traveled boldly down her new dress, noting every button, feminine ruffle, and sweet curve.

"Behave!" Though her voice remained at a whisper, it was a loud one.

"I'm trying to."

"Not very hard."

"Nobody will blame me when they find out. Trust me." He grinned down at her.

"That's it," she declared breathlessly. "I'm off to help Penelope and your mother."

He watched her glide away before he swaggered into the dining room to join the other men.

Bo angled his head at him, trying to get him to join him on his end of the bench. No doubt he was dying for an update with how things had gone between him and Eliza Jane last night. However, Keegan pretended not to notice. Instead, he clapped a hand on Jameson's arm and swung onto the bench beside him.

"What's the latest about that fire in the mountains?" Though his brother looked tired, Keegan wasn't surprised he was staying up to eat breakfast before heading to bed. His wife, Penelope, was an incredible cook, second only to Ma.

"We checked it out this morning. There were two sets of

hoof prints and two sets of boot prints. Both led up the mountain, roughly in the direction that the cattle rustler had described to the marshal. I think we finally located the trail he's been searching for."

"And they say eavesdroppers never hear anything good about themselves!" The very man they were speaking about popped his head around the doorway. Turner King's black top hat was tipped at a jaunty angle.

Jameson and Keegan stood in unison. "Come on in!" Jameson beckoned jovially at him to take a seat at the table with them.

"Don't mind if I do, gentlemen, especially since it sounds like you intend to put me to work right after breakfast." The marshal disappeared back into the hallway long enough to remove his hat and coat. Then he joined them in the dining room.

As if on cue, Penelope, Paloma, and Eliza Jane arrived from the kitchen. Their arms were full of platters heaped high with pancakes.

"Merry Christmas!" Penelope sang. Her gaze quickly came to rest on her husband.

"Merry Christmas, darling!" He blew a kiss at her, then tugged her head down for a real one after she set his plate in front of him.

"I love you," she murmured against his lips before straightening.

"I love you, too." He kept hold of her hand, forcing her to slide her fingers from his one by one on her return to the kitchen.

Chevy and Lance cheered at the sight of everything the women had prepared. Besides the pancakes, there were eggs, bacon, biscuits, and gravy. It was truly a feast.

The only two people missing this morning were Ethan and Annabelle. Ethan was still overseeing the range patrols, and

Annabelle probably didn't feel up to venturing out in the cold so early. Now that she was only a few short months from delivering her first babe, she was more cautious than ever.

Keegan was glad she'd remained at home. It meant Ethan would have someone to deliver a Christmas greeting to him when he arrived back after a long, cold night of work. Like Jameson, he'd catch a few hours of sleep. Then they'd all meet up for Christmas dinner later on.

After Jameson said a prayer of thanksgiving over their breakfast, the U.S. Marshal gave them a quick update on his investigation. "Another mail-order bride disappeared on her way to El Gato. This one hailed from Savannah. Like your six lovely brides from Atlanta, she was an heiress to a sizable fortune at one point in time. In an interesting development, her father's man of business turned out to be none other than Cane Fraser."

Keegan reached for Eliza Jane's hand beneath the table. As he threaded their fingers together, hers felt chilly with apprehension. "So this crooked man of business could be the connection between all the kidnappings and attempted kidnappings."

"That is my current theory. Right now, the evidence is circumstantial, but an associate of mine is bringing him in for questioning. We'll hopefully know more soon."

"In the meantime..." Jameson drawled in a hard voice. He went on to describe the fire burning on the mountainside last night and the discovery he and the range riders had made this morning. As he spoke, his wife ruffled her hand through the deep hat line etched into his hair. Before lowering her hand, she brushed at a mud stain on his collar.

"In the meantime," Turner King concluded, eyeing her movements with a bland expression, "you Fords are going to put every resource you have into keeping your wives safe while I do my job." There was a note of warning in his voice. "My men and I will follow that trail over yonder right after breakfast. I'm mighty grateful for the information you shared."

"You're welcome." Jameson leaned forward on the bench. "What can we do to help?"

"Just protect your wives and enjoy your Christmas." The marshal's voice was clipped.

Keegan cocked his head at him. "How many men do you have at your disposal?" He imagined it had been difficult to scrounge up much help on Christmas.

"Enough." The man's answer seemed unnecessarily curt, considering that it wasn't the first or even the second case they'd worked with him on. It was the third.

A little irritated by the fellow's prickliness, Keegan tried another tactic. "We've assisted you before, and we're more than happy to do it again." Since he was watching the marshal closely, he didn't miss the nearly imperceptible tightening of his jaw.

"In the past, you didn't have six brides to protect," the lawman returned evenly. "Thank you again for breakfast, ladies." He nodded his head respectfully at them. "I'm as full as a tick as you'd say in the south." He abruptly stood, his stance indicating that their conversation was coming to an end. However, he paused before exiting the room. "There is one thing you might be able to shed some light on for me. How in tarnation did you manage to marry six brides from the same town through the same bridal agency? I declare I've never seen the likes of it!"

I declare... Over yonder... As full as a tick as you'd say in the south... The man's words swirled in Keegan's head, along with the mental image of his very proper top hat. The only other folks he could recall using those exact phrases were the southern belles currently seated around the dining room table.

"I think I can answer that question." Paloma Clanton's musical voice wafted from the other end of the table.

Keegan waited until the marshal's head spun in her direction before half rising from his seat.

His mother briefly flicked her gaze to Keegan, long enough for him to give her a vehement head shake. He couldn't have explained why, but his gut was telling him to slow down on how much information they were feeding to Turner King.

His mother's gracious smile didn't change as she addressed the marshal. "It's quite simple, Mr. King." She rested her elbows conversationally on the table and leaned forward with her hands clasped against her cheek. "You can chalk it up to a mother's prayers."

Turner King looked puzzled. "I beg your pardon, ma'am?"

"A mother's prayers," she repeated, giving him a sublimely innocent look. "When my sons started searching for wives, I dropped to my knees and stayed there." She beamed a happy smile around the table. "Plus, my daughters-in-law happen to be close childhood friends. They kept up a constant stream of letters between here and Atlanta, hoping they'd end up in towns close enough to plan a reunion someday. This, my dear marshal, is what someday looks like." She spread her hands to take in all the young couples in her brood.

"The plans of the Lord stand firm forever." As Gray somberly quoted one of his favorite Psalms, adding his support to his wife's words, there was a steely note to his voice to match the frost at his temples. It was a tone that Keegan hadn't heard him employ often.

"You think the good Lord willed it, eh?" With a disbelieving shake of his head, Turner King spun around and headed for the front door.

Gray stood and followed him.

Keegan could hear them conversing quietly in the foyer. Then he saw Gray reach out to shake the marshal's hand. "God speed!" A moment later, the front door opened and shut.

Keegan relinquished Eliza Jane's hand and joined his stepfather at the front door. Together, they watched through the window as the marshal joined a group of six horsemen in the front yard.

"Is it my imagination, or did Turner King sound a bit like our southern belles over breakfast this morning?" Keegan rocked back on his heels, watching the marshal mount his horse.

"It's not your imagination, son." Gray's voice remained steely.

Something hard and heavy settled in Keegan's chest. "It certainly begs the question of who his associate in Savannah is."

"Your Ma has connections out that way," Gray reminded. "She might be able to shed some light on that."

Keegan nodded glumly. "I'm just going to throw this out there and follow it up by saying I hope it isn't true."

Gray folded his arms. "I'm afraid I already know what you're going to say, but let's hear it."

"Though it's never jumped out at me before, the marshal sounded like, looked like, and acted like a southerner this morning. He's clearly spent some time there. And now he's working on a criminal case here in Texas with an undeniable link to that same area. Even he would claim that's too much to be a coincidence."

Chapter 7: The Impossible

ELIZA JANE

Eliza Jane, who'd silently followed her husband to the foyer, froze at the accusation he was painting with his words.

Please don't let it be true, Lord. Her chest tightened with fear at the realization that both Keegan and his stepfather were questioning whether the U.S. Marshal was operating on the right side of the law.

She crept closer to the two men and reached for her husband's hand.

Though he glanced bleakly down at her, he didn't look surprised by her presence. He curled his hand possessively around hers and used it to tug her against his side. "We need to send word to El Gato and bring every able and willing man to Ford Ranch. Immediately!"

The fire in his gaze made her shiver. She knew it was his way of assuring her he would stop at nothing to protect her and her friends.

She tipped her head against his shoulder and mouthed the words *thank you*. She was grateful they'd had their long overdue heart-to-heart last night. Without meaning to, she'd given him more reason than ever to fight for her and their marriage.

Instead of answering, he bent his head to gently brush his lips against hers.

In the distance, Gray said something about heading back into the dining room to confer with his wife.

Once he left the foyer, Keegan deepened their kiss. He didn't lift his head until her tears dampened the fabric against his shoulder. "Don't cry, darling," he pleaded, looking worried.

"It's your fault." Though she sniffled, a smile trembled on her lips. "You make me feel things." Things she didn't think she would ever feel again.

"So long as that's all it is." He looked relieved. "I don't want you to be afraid, Eliza Jane. With all the trouble my brothers and I have faced, the Lord hasn't once failed us."

She admired his bravery, but a shiver still worked its way down her spine. "What if the marshal is dirty?"

"If he is, the truth will come to light. It always does."

"If he is, that makes him a very dangerous man."

"It's a good thing I fear God more than the likes of him." He sounded downright scoffing.

Eliza Jane gazed at him in amazement. His words underscored the fact that true wisdom didn't come from wealth, education, or social standing. He possessed none of those things, yet he was quite possibly the smartest person she'd ever met.

"Why are you looking at me like that?" He reached over to lightly tap her upturned nose.

"You're amazing, Keegan Ford."

He looked pleased. "What brought that on?"

"You're not afraid of much, are you?"

"Other than your safety? No."

"I'm really glad I married you."

His expression softened. "There are not many things I'd rather hear you say."

"Oh? What else would you like to hear me say?" She raised her head from his shoulder and batted her eyelashes at him.

"Someday, I'm going to tell you that I love you."

At her sharp intake of breath, he cuddled her closer to his side, not seeming to care that someone might walk in on them at any second. "And someday, you're going to say it back to me."

"I will?" she whispered, feeling like she was drowning beneath all of his dark-eyed intensity.

"That you will, darlin'."

His confidence made her heart tremble — in a good way, though.

CARLTON POKED HIS HEAD INTO THE FOYER TO inform them that Gray and Paloma were calling a family meeting in the living room. He made a few exaggerated kissing noises before ambling on down the hallway.

"I think everyone knows what we're doing out here," Eliza Jane murmured with a giggle.

"Who cares?" Keegan raised his eyebrows at her. "We're married. It's allowed."

"I care." She wrinkled her nose at him. "I suppose it's because this is so new."

"A good kind of new, I hope?" He dropped his arms.

"Yes," she whispered before twirling away from him.

It amused him to watch her rush into the living room ahead of him to join her friends by the Christmas tree. She was still so self-conscious about showing affection to him in front of others. Maybe it was a southern-girl sensibility. It didn't matter to him so long as she continued to be honest about her feelings when they were alone. He was thrilled with how much progress they'd made on their relationship in the last twenty-four hours alone.

He sent up a silent prayer as he gazed after her. *Thank you, Lord, for Eliza Jane. I will treasure your gift forever and always. Amen.*

A hard shoulder bumped his shoulder, and Bo's voice rumbled in his ear. "I'm trying to decide the most appropriate thing to say to you right now. I've been waffling between *you're welcome* and *I told you so.*"

Keegan used his shoulder to shove him back. "Aren't you ministers supposed to have a collection of more sanctimonious things to say?"

Bo raised and lowered his shoulders, giving him his meekest smile. "You know me. I've never been the pious type."

"True. You're more of the braggadocious buffoon type."

Bo grinned. "If that's your way of admitting I'm occasionally right about things, I'll take it."

Keegan snorted. "Fine. You were right about Eliza Jane."

"I know."

"There you go again." Keegan gave him another shoulder bump to throw him off balance so he could walk into the living room ahead of him.

Bo guffawed as he followed him. "Why are you hightailing it? We were having such a nice conversation."

"You were being smug."

"Bah! You're as happy as a pig in waller that I was right." Bo stuffed his hands in the pockets of his denim trousers, looking mighty pleased with himself.

"Is that the way you talk to your proper southern bride, mountain man?" Keegan mocked. "Always tooting your own horn?"

Bo leaned closer to confide in a loud whisper, "Not to brag, but we do more kissing than talking."

"That's bragging, alright."

Bo drew back, pretending to be offended. "There's just no pleasing you." He spoiled the insult with another unholy grin.

Keegan mockingly put up his fists. "You'd better be glad it's Christmas, and there are so many lovely ladies in the room. Otherwise, I might show you exactly where you can shove that smug look of yours."

Bo feigned a boxer's stance and bounced around Keegan on the balls of his feet.

"Mail run!" Annabelle Vasquez sailed into the room in a voluminous pinkish-orange gown, capturing everyone's attention with the letter she was waving.

There was a squeal of excitement from her friends as they jumped to their feet to fly in her direction.

"Actually, it's only one letter, and it's addressed to Eliza Jane." She handed it over.

Eliza Jane accepted it, scanned the envelope, and abruptly stuffed it inside her pocket.

"Who's it from?" Magnolia's eyes were wide with curiosity. Her red hair was tied back with a wide blue ribbon edged in white eyelet lace.

"Amelia Hudson." Eliza Jane's voice held no inflection.

Magnolia's lips tightened with disapproval. No one else asked any more questions, making Keegan wonder who Amelia Hudson was and why his wife's bevy of southern friends didn't seem to want to talk about her.

"Your dress is so pretty," Eliza Jane sighed, changing the subject. She reached for Annabelle to hold her at arm's length.

"It's not exactly a Christmas color." Annabelle wrinkled her nose wryly as she glanced down at her gown. The fabric was the shade of a sunrise, with an empire waist and more layers of lace than Keegan could count.

"You look like a Georgia peach," Eliza Jane assured with a quick hug. "Absolutely scrumptious!" She drew back, sniffing

COWBOY FOR ELIZA JANE

the air in delight. "You even smell like peaches. How in the world?"

"You noticed!" Annabelle's face lit up. "It's another one of my secret recipes. If you'd like a bottle—"

"I would absolutely *adore* a bottle," Eliza interrupted excitedly.

"Me, too," their friends chorused.

"Count me in," Paloma echoed, giving a girlish flutter of her hand. She was seated in an overstuffed chair by the Christmas tree. Gray was perched on the arm of it.

"Consider it done." Annabelle raised a hand to gesture at her husband, who was entering the room behind her. His arms were loaded with packages. "Here. Let me help you, sweetheart." She reached for a few of the packages, but he held them away from her.

"I'll handle the heavy lifting, Mrs. Vasquez." He winked at her. "You have enough to carry around these days."

While Annabelle pouted at him, her friends quickly converged on him. They had him stand by the tree while they divested his scarred hands of the many wrapped gifts and arrayed them artistically under the tree. Eliza Jane and Olivia Joy did the handing down part, while Magnolia and Emmaline remained on their knees, doing the arranging. Several of the packages were the same size and wrapped identically, making Keegan wonder if they contained bottles of the peach perfume Annabelle had promised her friends.

Eliza Jane eventually made her way to the sofa and took a seat on the edge of it. Keegan settled on the floor at her feet. Tipping his head back against the arm of the sofa, he pointedly eyed the tip of the envelope that was sticking out of her pocket. "Who's Amelia Hudson?"

To his chagrin, her face paled a few degrees. "The sister of the man I was once engaged to."

"I see." He searched her features, liking her honesty though not loving her answer.

"I'm afraid you don't." Eliza Jane leaned closer to him to mutter in a low voice, "She might very well be the most spiteful woman in the south. Since my father wasn't born wealthy, she never considered the Ferrells to be social equals to the Hudsons."

Ah. "I take it she didn't approve of her brother courting you."

"That's putting it mildly." Eliza Jane removed the envelope from her pocket, giving one corner of it a vicious twist, as if she'd like nothing better than to tear it to shreds. "There's nothing she could've possibly written me that I would ever want to read. I should toss her letter in the fire and be done with it."

The wheels of Keegan's mind were spinning in a different direction. "It's strange that she knew where to send the letter, don't you think?" He hoped his wife didn't think he was the kind of fellow who saw a bogeyman in every shadow, but even she had to admit that it was strange to receive a letter from someone she'd clearly made no effort to remain in touch with.

"You're right." Eliza Jane's lips tightened. "It's very strange, now that you mention it. I cannot begin to explain how she acquired my new address. Maybe I'll have to read her letter after all." With a sigh of resignation, she ripped open the envelope without finesse. She hastily scanned its contents, turned deathly pale, and allowed it to drop to her lap.

Keegan twisted around and rose to a crouch in front of her. "What did she say?"

Eliza Jane stared blankly at him for a moment. Her lips parted, and she tried to speak, but no sound came out. She gestured helplessly at the letter, making a small choking sound.

Scowling, he picked it up and skimmed the first two paragraphs.

Eliza Jane,

It gives me no joy to write to you, given my feelings on the topic of your involvement with my brother. After being presumed dead, however, Mark has defied all odds and straggled back home from the obscure town in Alabama where he's been convalescing. In short, he is now demanding to see you. He's in such critical condition that I didn't have the heart to deny his request. You certainly didn't make my job easy, though. I spent a small fortune tracking you down, only to discover you'd relocated to the most uncivilized corner of the country.

By the time you receive this letter, we'll be en route to Texas. May it weigh on your conscience for the rest of your days if your affianced does not survive our journey...

Keegan was unable to continue reading. Amelia Hudson gave new meaning to the word *spiteful*. His eyebrows felt like they were hanging from the ceiling. "Despite the small fortune she supposedly spent on finding you, it seems a little odd she doesn't know you're married," he muttered. Then again, someone as hateful as Amelia Hudson might've purposely ignored that detail.

His mother delicately cleared her throat from the other side of the room. "Are we ready to begin our meeting, or do you need more time over there, Keegan and Eliza Jane?"

Eliza Jane glanced blindly in her direction. "I, er..."

"What is it, hon?" Olivia Joy asked quickly. She ducked from beneath Bo's arm, where she'd been standing by the mantle, and hurried to her friend's side. "If that toxic little minx is trying to ruin your Christmas—"

"He's alive," Eliza Jane announced brokenly. "She claims Mark is alive."

"What?" Annabelle's voice rose in a small shriek from the opposite end of the sofa, making all heads turn in their direction. "He's been missing for two whole years!" Visibly agitated, she tweaked the skirt of her pinkish-orange gown.

"More like two-and-a-half years," Penelope snapped, looking equally incensed. "I'm not buying it."

"Me, either," Magnolia spat, shoving a handful of red hair over one shoulder. "Mark my words, that horrible creature is up to something."

Keegan watched Eliza Jane's face crumple further at her friends' reactions. "Whoa!" he cautioned, holding up his hands to stall any further commentary. His wife looked close to passing out. "We have no reason to doubt the truth behind this woman's claims."

"On the contrary," Annabelle's voice was bitter, "we have every reason to doubt her. Believe me when I say she'd rather her brother remain dead than see him reunited with—"

"Annabelle, please," he begged.

At his horrified expression, she seemed to collect herself. "Please accept my apologies," she cried in an agonized voice. "You're right, Keegan. I should've held my tongue. I don't know what I was thinking." She moved closer to Eliza Jane on the sofa. "Oh, my dearest friend! I can only imagine what's going through your mind right now!"

For an answer, Eliza Jane collapsed into her arms.

Keegan watched her in alarm. She hadn't so much as shed a tear over the news that her former beau was still alive. She was as limp as a wet leaf. It was as if all her energy had drained out of her.

His brain raced ahead to other matters, like the fact that he and Eliza Jane hadn't gotten around to consummating their marriage yet. Technically, she could still annul their marriage if she wanted to.

Did she?

Would she?

He hadn't realized he was crumpling the letter from

Amelia Hudson in his fist until Bo walked across the living room to take it from him. Keegan managed to catch a glimpse of a detail he hadn't previously noticed before the letter left his hand.

It was dated the first week of December. *That's impossible!* He made a swipe for the letter, and Bo handed it back. "Something's wrong. Her letter is dated before you departed Atlanta."

Eliza Jane twisted in Annabelle's arms to give him a pitiful look. "Maybe it's a mistake." She fished blindly on the sofa cushion beside her for the envelope. Holding it out to him, she quavered, "What does the postmark say?"

He flipped over the torn envelope. "The same thing." His heartbeat thudded with apprehension. Something felt off about the whole situation.

A bit of color returned to Eliza Jane's lips as she struggled to sit up again. "Why would Amelia lie about something like that?"

Annabelle's rosy lips twisted bitterly. "I can think of a number of reasons and none of them good. Magnolia's right. That troublemaker is up to something." Her voice shook with anger.

Eliza Jane raised a hand to her throat, looking ill. "Even if there's a logical explanation to the date that we don't yet understand, one thing is for sure. Amelia and Mark could arrive in Texas any day. Any minute, for that matter." She swayed dizzily on the sofa cushion.

Magnolia pursed her lips thoughtfully. "If they left Atlanta before we did, they should actually already be here."

A faint moan escaped Eliza Jane.

"That's it!" Keegan stood. "My wife and I need a moment. Alone." He cast a dark look around the room, warning them not to contradict him. "Feel free to carry on with your meeting and fill us in on the details later."

Without waiting for an answer, he scooped his bride into his arms and carried her from the room. Moving with her down the hallway to the back of the house, he found the perfect spot to continue their conversation — a divan beside a wall of books in the back parlor. Covered in blue velvet, it was the fanciest piece of furniture in the house. His mother had ordered it from a special catalogue at the General Store in El Gato.

He sat with her in his lap, not liking how boneless she felt. She was draped against his chest like a rag doll. Settling his chin on the top of her head, he simply held her.

Though she didn't weep audibly, he felt the trickle of warm tears against his neck.

His heart ached for her. As he continued to hold her, he searched his mind for something to say that might offer a ray of comfort. "Do you remember what I said about telling you I love you some day?"

She grew still. Then she slowly nodded.

"It's true. I'm falling in love with you."

Though she caught her lower lip between her teeth, she still didn't speak.

"I wanted you to know, in the event you have to make a difficult decision in the coming days." *Like whether to annul our marriage.*

"I'm married to you," Eliza Jane whispered.

Keegan wondered if he'd imagined her words. "Did you say—?"

"Yes." She curled a hand in the fabric of his shirt. "We said our vows before God and the people we love the most. I've been living with you ever since. I've lost track of the number of times we've kissed. I bear your name." Her voice grew thick with emotion. "I'm a Ford now."

"I've been sleeping on the couch, darlin'. According to our marriage contract, you have every right to—"

"You chose to sleep on the couch," she interrupted fiercely, sitting up to face him. "I never asked you to."

He threaded his hands through her hair, cupping the back of her head. "Eliza Jane, are you trying to tell me—?"

"Yes," she said simply.

He tipped his head back against the back of the divan, feeling weak with relief. "If you're trying to make a grown man cry from sheer happiness, it's working." *Good gravy!* He wasn't exaggerating. His eyes were damp, and his heart was overflowing.

"It's your fault for marrying a complete hoyden." Her voice grew stronger even as more tears streaked her face. "I keep trying to warn you, but you never listen."

With a cry of exultation, he gathered her close again, this time to seal his mouth over hers. He felt like a man dying of thirst who'd finally crawled his way to the edge of a water hole. His very soul was reaching out to touch hers.

Despite the darkness hanging over Ford Ranch, he felt like he was bathing in his own personal slice of sunlight. Later, much later when he could speak again, he repeated the words burning in his mouth and on his heart. "I love you, Eliza Jane Ford." Though he didn't expect her to say them back, he needed her to understand that every part of his heart was hers for the taking when she was ready.

"I love you, too, Keegan."

He smoothed her hair back from her damp face, anxiously searching her features. "You don't have to say it yet. I wasn't expecting—"

"Yes, I do, because it's true." More tears scalded her cheeks. "It wasn't supposed to happen so soon. It hardly makes any sense to me, but it did happen. You happened."

Her confession was the most incredible gift anyone had ever given him. To have his bride hand her heart to him on

Christmas day, of all days, felt like the ultimate gift — one that could never be topped.

A knock sounded on the front door of the house. It was so loud that it resounded all the way down the hallway, reaching their ears.

For reasons he couldn't explain, Keegan's hand went to one of the guns in his holster. He gently slid his wife from his lap and transferred her to the cushion beside him. "We weren't expecting any more visitors today." Turner King and his men were the only ones, and they'd left for the mountains more than an hour ago.

They heard the front door open and Gray's voice boom. "I wasn't expecting you back so soon, marshal."

Keegan and Eliza Jane stood at the same time, staring in puzzlement at each other. Why had the dirty marshal returned?

"Stay behind me," he muttered, moving into the hallway. He hugged the wall, keeping his wife in the shadows as long as he could.

"This was unexpected for me, too, Mr. Clanton." Turner King stepped into the foyer, though Gray hadn't precisely invited him inside. He gestured to a man and woman who'd been standing behind him. Though they were bundled in coats and scarves up to their eyeballs, they were shaking from the cold. "As it turns out, the fire on the mountain wasn't a pair of bandits like we'd feared. They are friends from Atlanta, trying to find their way to Ford Ranch."

"Whose friends?" Gray inquired slowly.

"Friends of your sons' wives, of course." The marshal sounded a tad irritable over being made to elaborate.

Keegan's gaze dropped to the feet of Eliza Jane's so-called friends. Only one of them was wearing the kind of boots that would've left the footprints on the mountain his oldest brother had encountered. The woman, on the other hand, was wearing a pair of lace-up shoes with tiny pointed heels. They most definitely did not match the second set of footprints they'd found.

"Where is she?" the woman spat, stepping across the threshold and tearing the scarf from her face. A plain-faced creature emerged with pinched features and malice dripping from her eyes. "I'm looking for Eliza Jane Ferrell."

Gray didn't budge from his stance in the doorway, forcing the woman to walk around him. "There isn't anyone here by that name."

"Nonsense!" She stomped across the entry foyer, her dark beady gaze darting in and out of every corner. Finally glancing down the hallway, she pointed past Keegan's shoulder. "There she is!"

Gray followed her outstretched arm. "Ah. You must be referring to Eliza Jane Ford, my daughter-in-law."

"Pshaw!" Amelia Hudson's heels click-clacked down the hardwood floor as she confronted Eliza Jane. Or attempted to.

Keegan stepped in her path, barring her way. "I'm Keegan Ford, Eliza Jane's husband. And you are?"

"Oh, for pity's sake," the woman snarled. "I'm Amelia Hudson, the sister of her affianced. I must have heard you wrong, because she and my brother, Mark, were very much still betrothed when she left Atlanta."

Chapter 8: Mountain Smoke

ELIZA JANE

"Perhaps we should take this, er, reunion into the living room," Gray suggested mildly.

Eliza Jane was more than ready to be seated again. Her knees were threatening to crumble beneath her as she strove to get a glimpse of the man she'd once been betrothed to.

Though she certainly had no intention of renewing her engagement with him now that she was wed, it was truly a miracle he was still alive! She was still absorbing the shock of it. Questions swam through her mind about what he had suffered during the war, and why it had taken him so long to return to his family. If he'd returned even a month sooner than now, her future might have taken a very different turn indeed!

Amelia held her head in the same haughty manner Eliza Jane remembered as she unbuttoned her coat and untied her scarf. Her expression was sour and her attitude so superior that it took an extra moment for Eliza Jane to additionally note the bedraggled state of her gown. Though the gold high-necked ensemble had once been elegant, it was now as faded and patched as the black mourning gown Eliza Jane had worn for so long.

She wore it like a queen, however. She acted like one, too, practically throwing her coat and scarves at Gray without bothering to look back and see if he caught them.

He did, of course, hanging them on the hall tree without comment.

She glided over to help her companion, who remained stooped over a cane on the entrance rug.

Only when she removed his hat and unwound his scarf did Eliza Jane finally get a good look at his face.

It wasn't Mark Hudson at all! Or was it? Confusion swam through her, tightening her throat.

If the stranger standing in front of the door was truly the miracle Amelia claimed he was, she certainly hadn't exaggerated his condition one bit. Mark Hudson was teetering at death's door. His pallor was a ghastly shade beneath the thick black patch covering his left eye. His shaggy, overgrown hair covered most of his other eye and was in desperate need of a trim. The rest of his face was riddled with scars, making him virtually unrecognizable. He could've been Mark Hudson or any other man his approximate height and build.

His head jerked as he caught sight of her with his one good eye. "Eli-za J-Jane?" He took a hitching step in her direction. "Is it r-really you?" he stammered.

She nodded without answering, remaining partially hidden behind her husband's shoulder. It was impossible to read Mark's expression, since his face remained downcast. Though she'd never been accused of being a coward, there was something about his scarred visage that made it harder for her to breathe.

There was nothing familiar to her about him. Nothing whatsoever that struck a chord in her memory. If she'd passed him on the street, she wouldn't have recognized him. They might as well have been strangers.

Keegan kept her as far from their uninvited guests as possible, holding back to allow the brother and sister to walk into the living room ahead of them. After entering the room, he parked her in the chair nearest the doorway in the event they needed to make a quick exit.

Gray cleared the sofa of its current occupants with a silent jerk of his head, yielding it to their three guests. It placed them in the dead center of the room, surrounded by the Ford brothers, Bo, and Ethan. Every cowboy in the room was armed and making no effort to hide it.

"Merry Christmas," Amelia Hudson trilled, seeking out Eliza Jane again with her gaze. Despite her words, there wasn't a drop of holiday cheer visible in her expression.

"What do you want, Amelia?" Eliza Jane saw no point in beating around the bush.

"As much as it pains me, I was hoping to unite my brother with the woman he loves." Amelia settled the skirt of her faded dress around her ankles. It boasted a double row of military-style buttons across the bodice and matching silver buttons at her wrists.

"It's touching that you traveled so far to pay me a visit." Eliza Jane tried to catch Mark's gaze again, but failed.

He was either refusing to meet her eye or didn't have the energy to fully lift his head.

"It's a miracle, you mean!" Amelia's voice was sharp with indignation. "I am taken aback that you aren't happier to see him."

Eliza Jane swallowed hard. Maybe her heart was numb from shock, because she felt nothing each time her gaze landed on the man. "In your letter, you mentioned Mark has been living in Alabama—"

"Convalescing," the woman corrected abrasively. "He was fighting for his life on a small farm in Newhope."

Eliza Jane frowned at the name of the town. Though she'd received high marks in geography during her grammar school days, she'd never before heard of that particular town. It sounded made up to her.

"I'm unfamiliar with the place," she murmured politely. "Where in Alabama did you say it was?"

"Oh, for pity's sake! Why does it matter?" Amelia straightened her spine. "Everyone knows Alabama is full of places that don't appear on a map. The state itself barely appears on a map."

"So, how have you been?" Eliza Jane returned her attention to the man Amelia claimed was her brother and found him ready to nod off to sleep.

"As I said in my letter, Mark is not well." Amelia curled her arm protectively around the man. "Sadly, our trip was even more difficult on him than I anticipated. He was fortunate to..." She sighed and didn't finish the sentence. "I'm just glad we made it." She abruptly concluded their visit only moments later.

Turner King stood and escorted them back to the foyer to retrieve their coats.

A wagon awaited them at the base of the porch steps to carry them away, presumably to El Gato.

"We'll be in touch," Amelia promised cryptically on their way out the front door.

A stunned silence settled over the farmhouse after she and her brother were driven away by the marshal.

"Well, that was strange!" Annabelle shook her head. She was sitting in the overstuffed chair next to Paloma. Ethan was sitting on the arm of it the same way Gray was sitting on the arm of his wife's chair.

"You can say that again," Olivia Joy noted quietly.

"Shall we get back to our meeting?" Paloma suggested after a stilted pause.

Jameson was leaning against the wall beside the pianoforte, frowning into the distance like he was thinking hard about something. "Maybe I'm too tired to think clearly since I'm only operating on a couple hours of sleep here, but humor me." He steepled his fingers together as he laid out his thoughts. "Assuming their whole surprise visit was nothing more than the cock and bull it felt like, what did they hope to accomplish by coming here?"

Keegan shared his oldest brother's sentiments to a T. "They got a good look at the layout of the farmhouse and everyone in it."

Bo nodded in agreement. He and Olivia Joy were standing by the mantle again. His arm was draped loosely around her shoulders. "Exactly. And they traipsed through the west side of Ford Ranch on their way here. Probably got a count of the outbuildings. Might've even sized up the herds."

"Again. Why?" Jameson demanded.

Keegan didn't like the possibilities that popped into his head, but it was a fair question. "I think we have something they want."

"You mean someone," Penelope corrected fiercely. She was perched on the pianoforte bench beside her husband. "Several someones, in fact."

"So what are we going to do about it?" Jameson unsteepled his hands and lowered them to his sides.

Paloma cocked her head in consideration. "Gray and I have already started composing a series of telegrams to fire off to J.R. Hubert & Sons. They're a reputable law firm with extensive contacts throughout the south, which is why I chose them to represent The Western Moon Agency. I'm confident they'll be able to uncover the information we seek about Cane Fraser."

It was a good start. Eliza Jane felt the first stirring of hope.

Penelope gave an excited bounce on the pianoforte bench. "Ethan has no less than three staggered pairs of riders on their way to El Gato as we speak. Yes, it leaves us a few men short during daylight hours, but we should have reinforcements galore arriving here by nightfall. Our friends in town will not fail us."

"They left at different times and took different routes." Ethan traced an invisible map in the air to explain the routes. "They know this area like the backs of their hands. Even the marshal and his posse won't be able to out think them, out ride them, or out shoot them if it comes to that." His handsome Hispanic features settled into grim lines. "We pray that it doesn't."

Eliza Jane's heart tightened at the realization that the Fords and their most trusted staff members weren't taking any chances. They'd fully anticipated their first team of riders being intercepted and had carefully crafted a Plan B and a Plan C.

"What are we going to do about the marshal?" If they'd already discussed the possibility that the lawman was corrupt, they'd done it in her and Keegan's absence earlier.

"His credentials are legitimate, if that's what you're asking." Jameson's expression was troubled. "In the past, he impressed me as a straight shooter. We assisted him with a couple of cases and worked really well together."

"Technically, it was three," Keegan reminded. "We shared what we knew about those cattle rustlers when we first arrived in town."

Jameson let out a heavy breath. "The rustlers have been an ongoing problem. Not for us, since we're so well staffed, but for some of the other ranchers."

"All too true." Keegan stabbed a finger in the air to punctuate his brother's statement. "They've been complaining for months about the marshal's lack of progress in addressing the problem."

"Months?" Eliza repeated. "What has he been doing during that time?" She felt like they might be on to something.

Keegan shrugged. "Other than developing a bad attitude? Not much, it seems."

"Maybe he's changed," she mused. Maybe the marshal had been operating on both sides of the law lately.

"Jameson's right," Annabelle volunteered tiredly. "Turner King has done us a number of good turns."

"Such as?" Eliza Jane pressed.

"Well, for one thing, he arrested Garth Swingler and Dale Featherfall, who followed me here from Atlanta." She shuddered at the memory. "Garth had me tied to the railroad tracks, trying to force me to marry the horrid Mr. Featherfall — all to get their hands on my father's railroad spur. The marshal was one of the last ones to give up trying to set me free before the train ran me down. The second-to-last one, to be exact. My husband never gave up on me, which is why I'm still here." She gazed fondly up at him.

Ethan reached for her hand and lifted it to his lips. "I will be forever grateful for the marshal's help that day."

Penelope waved a hand to jump into the conversation next. "He arrested my black-hearted Uncle Mort and Dalton Gentry, the foppish goon he tried to force me to marry."

Jameson nodded. "We're mighty grateful to him, as well, for carting those two scoundrels off to jail."

Magnolia and Emmaline, who'd moved to sit on the sofa after the Hudsons' departure, started whispering. They leaned their heads closer to examine something on the cushion behind Magnolia's head.

Eliza Jane watched them curiously. "Is everything alright over there?"

"I'm not sure." Magnolia swiped at a spot on the sofa. The tip of it came back gray. She sniffed at it. "I think it's paint."

"On my sofa?" Penelope groaned, half-rising from the pianoforte bench.

"I believe so." Magnolia sniffed at her finger. "Yes, it's definitely paint. Isn't this about where Mark Hudson was sitting?"

Eliza Jane nodded, frowning. "Is my memory failing me, or was there absolutely nothing familiar about that man?"

Annabelle grimaced. "Please don't get me started down that road. I'm trying to be respectful of your feelings. We all are," she sighed, smoothing the skirt of her gown.

"I know you are, and I adore you for it," Eliza Jane assured quickly. "But let's face it, all six of us have known Mark Hudson since we were knee-high to grasshoppers. He was polished and well-spoken."

"And snobby," Annabelle muttered beneath her breath.

Eliza ignored her comment. "He wore Italian suits," she continued quietly, "and was ever the perfect gentleman."

"His tastes were foppish and silly, you mean." A giggle escaped Annabelle, then another. "Every time he pranced your way with his foolish walking stick, I wanted to snatch it out of his hands and wrap it around his ears."

"You mean he always walked with a cane?" Keegan gazed curiously between the two women.

"Not because he needed to. He only used one back then to be stylish," Eliza Jane explained, shaking her head at Annabelle when her friend burst into another round of giggles.

"If you say so." Keegan still looked so puzzled that Annabelle laughed all the harder.

Eliza Jane rolled her eyes at them and pointed at the paint-spattered couch. "What disturbed me the most about the man sitting next to Amelia Hudson earlier was the fact that he refused to meet my gaze. Maybe I'm being insensitive about his condition, but he didn't seem to take any joy in seeing me again. He made no effort to embrace me. He didn't renew any previous declarations of his affections. He was...utterly vacant."

It made her heart ache all over again to put her concerns

into words. Out of the corner of her eye, she watched her husband's shoulders grow stiff. "The Mark Hudson I once knew..." She stopped and cleared her throat. "That wasn't him," she concluded regretfully.

Keegan bent his head to stare at his hands.

"You're right. It wasn't," Magnolia declared, bending to examine the newest spot of paint her sister had discovered.

"You found more paint, I presume?" Penelope propped her elbows on the pianoforte and dropped her chin in her hands. "The sofa is probably ruined."

Emmaline nodded, wrinkling her nose. "Whoever was sitting next to Amelia earlier was wearing a lot of paint," she announced, holding up two fingers. She pointed at the first one. "This spot is the pale gray color of those scars lining his hands. And this one," she wiggled a second finger in the air, "is that putrid greenish pallor staining his cheeks."

"It's theatrical paint," Magnolia concluded in a triumphant voice. "We should know. We cut our teeth on the seats at our father's opera house."

Emmaline nodded, adopting a faraway look. "We used to play tag in the auditorium and hide-n-seek through the dressing rooms. When Father wasn't looking, we played dress-up with the costumes of the singers and took turns painting each other's faces." Her expression sharpened again. "That's why I know what I'm talking about when I say this." She pointed at the sofa. "Someone tried very hard to make the man sitting here look like a wounded soldier, but it was only paint. I'm sorry, but that all but guarantees he wasn't Mark Hudson."

A stunned silence met her words.

Eliza Jane's shoulders slumped in relief. The number of emotions she'd experienced in the past hour had brought her to the brink of exhaustion. At this very moment, though, she was just glad her friends didn't think she was crazy for insisting the man who'd come to visit her wasn't who he said he was.

Keegan slowly raised his head to meet his wife's gaze.

She clung to it for an emotion-charged moment.

Without dropping her gaze, he inquired of no one in particular, "Why in the world would Amelia Hudson bring someone posing as her brother to Ford Ranch?"

"Why do criminals do anything?" Jameson mused slowly.

"It's about the money. It's always about the money." Keegan's mouth twisted with anger. "They couldn't have cared less about the agony their game might stir in my wife's heart."

She hastened to assure him. "I'm alright, Keegan." She stood to face him, no longer concerned about hiding her feelings for him from her friends. "More than I've been in a long time, I think." She stepped closer to him, and his arms came around her. She leaned her head against his shoulder, craving his nearness and strength. "I felt nothing but pity and disgust for them."

He pressed his cheek to the top of her head. "I'm still less than thrilled about their visit. I could see the toll it was taking on you."

"It's over now." Another thought struck her. "But we learned something while they were here. Something significant that can't be overlooked."

When no one spoke, she raised her head from her husband's shoulder. "It means Turner King is dirty. Maybe he was once an honest lawman. From the way you described him, it certainly sounds as if he used to be, but there's no denying his compliance in today's shenanigans. Amelia Hudson brought an imposter into our midst, and the marshal allowed it."

Emmaline rolled her eyes. "He wasn't even a good actor," she complained. "I could put on a far more convincing act in a simple game of charades. No theatrical paint necessary, though it's quite entertaining to wear it."

"That I would like to see sometime." Redding studied his bride in fascination, as if trying to imagine her wearing face paint.

"Oh, I've seen and heard both Magnolia and Emmaline in action, and they can put on a performance that will leave you spellbound," Eliza Jane affirmed merrily. "Even in a simple game of charades. I'm not sure if cowboys are into parlor games, but if you are..." She was rewarded with smiles of beaming gratitude from the sisters.

Bo waved two fingers in the air. "I, for one, can hold my own in charades."

Keegan smirked across the room at him, unable to imagine the mountain man playing such a silly game. "Acting like a buffoon, you mean?"

Eliza Jane was relieved to see her husband's humor restored. Though he'd never admit it, Amelia Hudson's visit had been every bit as hard on him as it had been on her. "What about you, Mr. Ford?" She tipped her head back to gaze teasingly up at him. "Are you too manly for charades, or would you be willing to serve as my partner?"

He shook his head at her, chuckling instead of answering.

"Oh, come on! You're my one and only partner, Keegan Ford. If you don't like it, you shouldn't have married a complete—"

"Hoyden?" He swooped in to steal a kiss from her in front of everyone, making her blush and laugh and blush some more.

"It's Christmas," she wheedled. "It wouldn't kill you to play one teensy little game."

He winked at the others and kissed her again. "Sorry, folks. It's the only method I've found effective in silencing my wife."

Eliza Jane swatted his shoulder, but ultimately ended up kissing him back.

The revelry in the room soon led to a gift unwrapping session. She was delighted to discover a bottle of Annabelle's perfume under the tree for her. "It smells so wonderful," she sighed, uncapping it and sniffing it happily. "Just like the trees in our backyard where I grew up." She shot a wistful look at her husband, who was on his knees beside her in front of the tree. "Can you even grow peaches here in Texas?"

He looked amused. "I've never tried, but I'm willing to give it a shot for my favorite hoyden."

The next gift Eliza Jane opened was a bolt of cheery blue-and-white checkered gingham. Packaged with it was a ball of delicately crocheted lace. "Keegan!" She spun his way, clutching his lovely gifts against her bosom. "How did you know I love gingham so much?"

He angled a thumb at her friends. "I might've received a few helpful hints."

She laid down the precious gifts to throw her arms around his neck. "Thank you! Thank you! Thank you!" She hugged him tightly, reveling in the adoring look in his eyes.

Her gift to him wasn't nearly as exciting in comparison, but it was all she'd been able to pull off during the few days leading up to Christmas. She'd embroidered longhorn steers on the outer flaps of two matching pillowcases. She'd stitched a pine bow garland beneath them to add a bit of holiday flair to the scene.

"These are far more my style, darlin'." He grinned in approval down at them.

"As opposed to...?" She taunted playfully.

"Charades." He winked at her.

The room erupted into laughter. Before it quieted, he leaned closer to speak directly in her ear. "Correct me if I'm wrong, Mrs. Ford, but these appear to be a matched set of pillowcases."

"Yes." She was happy that he'd noticed. It was with great reluctance that she said goodbye to him after lunch. She walked with him to the door as he shrugged on his coat and prepared to take his next guard shift at the boarding house. "This has been the most wonderful Christmas!" She gazed adoringly at him. "I wish you didn't have to head back out in the cold."

He brushed a thumb beneath her chin. "Any chance you'll draw me another bath to thaw me out when I get back?"

"There's definitely a chance." She intended to have the newly embroidered pillowcases on their bed, a candle in the window, and a fire in the hearth.

"What did I ever do to deserve you?" He dipped his head to touch his forehead to hers.

"That's an odd thing to ask a hoyden," she murmured against his lips.

A laugh rumbled through his chest. "My very own hoyden." His voice grew husky. "I'm never going to give you up, you know."

"Please don't."

"I'll confess I was a little worried earlier when you first showed me that letter."

"You have nothing to worry about," she declared softly. "You're stuck with me, cowboy, until the end of your days."

He touched his mouth to hers in the tenderest of kisses. "I love you, Mrs. Ford. So much."

"I love you, too. Hurry back to me," she whispered.

"I'll be counting the minutes." With one last lingering kiss, he reached for his Stetson on the hall tree and slapped it on his head. Then he opened the door and stepped into the icy wind.

KEEGAN WAS ACCOMPANIED BY A PAIR OF RANGE riders like Jameson had been the night before. There was too much at stake. He and his brothers weren't taking any chances. Jameson rode to the construction site a few hours later to inform him that their reinforcements had started to trickle in from El Gato. By mid-afternoon, that trickle had turned into a steady flow. By the time Keegan's shift ended at nightfall, the flow amounted to over thirty extra ranch hands and range riders.

Thank you, Lord! Keegan's faith soared. He was more confident than ever that the danger surrounding Ford Ranch would soon be over. While the marshal had spent the last several months assembling his crooked posse, the Fords had done little more than snap their fingers and had managed to throw together a full-blown militia in a matter of hours.

More men on horseback were still arriving. Ethan and Jameson met them on the front lawn, gave them their marching orders, and divided them into teams. It was a good thing they'd finished rebuilding their three-story barn a month earlier, because the lofts were able to double as makeshift dorm rooms.

As it turned out, there was a nice side perk to calling in reinforcements from El Gato. It provided the perfect opportunity to start spreading the word about the land they had up for sale and rent in El Vaquero. News about the available lots on Main Street spread among their guests like wildfire. When Jameson rode out to relieve Keegan and start his second shift, roughly half the homestead acreage was spoken for by prospective buyers and renters. It was only a matter of hours before the holiday ended and the bank, attorney's office, and land office reopened in El Gato. They expected to have their first official contracts in hand shortly afterward.

A wide smile stretched across Keegan's face as he stomped up the porch steps of home. A flicker of light on the distant mountain gave him pause as he reached for the handle of the front door.

He frowned at the glow of flames and swirl of smoke rising skyward. It was yet more proof that the marshal had lied. Amelia Hudson and her imposter brother hadn't been brought to Ford Ranch from the mountains. Whoever had been squatting out there last night was still squatting out there tonight.

Though Jameson was probably looking at the same scene right now, Keegan hastily hunted down Ethan to report what he'd seen. Ethan assured him he was already tracking the fire. "Once we finish assembling our reinforcements, we're going to ride out there and route them out ourselves," he announced grimly. "No more waiting on the crooked marshal to make his move."

"Count me in." Keegan was glad all over again to have the most ruthless range rider in the west in their employ. It wasn't his job to round up criminals, but he'd get the task done, anyway.

"I appreciate that." Ethan angled his head toward Keegan's cabin. "Now go enjoy your last few hours of Christmas, my friend."

Keegan tipped his hat at him and took off at a jog.

As promised, Eliza Jane had a warm bath waiting for him in the kitchen and another warm fire waiting in their bedroom afterward. She also had an unlimited supply of kisses stored up from his favorite hoyden.

Chapter 9: Storm Watch

KEEGAN

January

The New Year arrived in a swirl of frost, followed by a fresh blanket of snow. Flurries were still falling as Keegan rode to the construction site. His horse's hooves were the first thing to churn through the field of perfect whiteness.

His younger brothers and Bo arrived only a few minutes behind him. Bo had walked, but his brothers had ridden. While they tethered their horses next to his at the new hitching post, Keegan glanced up at the new roof covering the boarding house. They'd worked until sundown yesterday to hammer the last cedar shingles into place. With the threat of more snow coming, they'd wanted the building under its roof as soon as possible.

Bo grabbed his tools and headed to the back of the boarding house, where he'd been sawing and sanding doors and window frames for the past few days with Lance and Chevy's assistance. Keegan could soon hear the steady scrape of their saws, along with the occasional pithy comments his two youngest brothers made about, well, everything.

Jameson tromped past Keegan, muffling a yawn. He'd pulled the night shift again. "I'm about ready to head back. Do you need to update me on anything before I take off?"

Keegan shook his head, reaching for his hammer. "Not unless you spotted another fire on the mountain."

He stepped back to survey the front outer wall that he, Colton, and Redding would be working on this morning. They'd cut and sanded a pile of long cedar planks to use as siding. It was sturdy, and it would go up fast. They planned to add an outer layer of adobe after it set and weathered a bit.

"I didn't." Jameson muffled another yawn. "It's been pretty quiet on the mountain for the past twelve hours, give or take. Who knows? Maybe they took a break from spying on us. A late holiday or something."

"Don't know. Don't care. We'll be ready when they return." Keegan doubted the thugs would be gone for long. His gut told him they were gunning for a confrontation soon. He was surprised they'd held off as long as they had. Then again, Ford Ranch was crawling with range riders these days. Maybe their heightened level of security was giving their enemies second thoughts.

"We will certainly be ready." Jameson looked every bit as confident as Keegan felt. "One of Bo's mountain friends stopped by late last night after work. He plans to sign a contract to buy some land from us tomorrow. I sent him to Andrew to draw up the paperwork. Claims he's been looking for the right spot for months to open up shop."

"If Bo can vouch for him, that's good enough for me." Keegan eyed the pile of siding, anxious to get started. "What sort of business is he in?"

"One we're in sore need of." His brother's tired features stretched into a grin. "Looks like we've got ourselves a black-smith," he crowed.

They leaned in to slap each other on the back. It was a

victory, indeed. Blacksmiths tended to run on the big side, both them and their apprentices. Not only would they bring a much-needed service to El Vaquero, they would also bring some much-needed muscle. Any two-bit outlaw riding through town would think twice before picking a fight with a man who pounded iron for a living.

"Oh, and the Pickens brothers want to open a sawmill. Plus, Old Man Brown wants first dibs on the feed mill for his grandsons. Says he'll oversee the operation and turn it over to them when they're ready."

"And Gray's got the livery covered. It's coming together just like we envisioned." Keegan glanced back toward Ford Ranch, knowing their stepfather would be joining them any minute now. He usually arrived at the construction site an hour or two later than the others and brought breakfast. Paloma's rules. It was her way of making sure her husband didn't overdo it, since he was twice the age of her sons.

Jameson rubbed his gloved hands together and stomped his boots to stay warm. "Ma says she's just about got Andrew Emerson talked into relocating his law office out here, too. She thinks he'll sign if we turn over the land office duties to him. It would give him all the business he needs to get started." He chuckled, shaking his head. "It's not like he doesn't handle most of that for us already."

Keegan had certainly been hoping in that direction. "That's really good news. I know Ma has been pulling every trick out of her bag to recruit him. And if we do—"

"You mean when," Jameson corrected, pulling the brim of his Stetson lower to protect his face from the icy mountain breeze.

"Yes, and it'll snowball from there." Keegan picked up the first piece of siding and held it in the air so he could see how it was going to look against the front of the boarding house. "Andrew will want a bank, post office, and telegraph service nearby." Fortunately, the esquire had the kinds of connections it would take to make those things happen. Their mother was wise to work so hard on getting him to invest in their town. Andrew's support was pivotal for attracting the other businesses they would need to have in place soon. A general store, apothecary, and gunsmith were also high on their wishlist. Their brides were additionally hoping for a tailor, hatter, and shoemaker.

A companionable silence settled between the brothers as they gazed around them, each dreaming their own dreams. They were facing what would eventually be the living room of the boarding house. Or maybe it was supposed to be the parlor. Keegan wasn't quite sure what his wife intended to call it yet. All he knew was that it would serve as a receiving room of sorts — the first room their guests would step into when they entered the boarding house. Eliza Jane planned to have a check-in booth on one side of the room, plus a fireplace and a scattering of chairs on the other. According to her, it needed to be well lit and inviting.

It needs to feel like a handshake, she'd said. Colorful words, but Keegan understood what she meant by them.

"Alright, then. I'm heading home for breakfast. Penelope is probably wondering what's taking me so long." Jameson spun in a slow circle to survey their progress on the boarding house one last time. He looked pleased. They all were. The outer walls would be completed or nearly completed by the end of the day. Then it would only be a matter of installing the interior cabinetry, ceilings, floors, and adding the furnishings. At the rate they were going, the boarding house could be up and running for business as soon as February.

"Go! We'll talk more over dinner." Keegan went to work, hammering the first piece of siding in place. He heard Jameson ride off, but the sound of a horse galloping in their direction soon followed. Knowing it was probably Gray with breakfast,

Keegan finished hammering his board into place, then laid down his hammer.

Gray rode into view and leaped off his Mustang before it came to a complete halt. His expression instantly put Keegan on alert.

"What's wrong?" He jogged in his stepfather's direction.

"Our riders just returned from El Gato with a whole pile of bad news from Andrew," Gray wheezed, bending over double to slap his hands against his knees.

Keegan frowned and waited for his stepfather to catch his breath. They'd been sending range riders to town daily to keep up the flow of information between them and their family attorney.

"Here's the skinny of it. Turner King is no longer our friend. It's possible he's never been our friend." When Gray straightened, his face was drawn with worry. "At this point, we're not even sure he's a real marshal."

When Keegan started to protest, he held up his hands. "I know. I know. The fellow's got credentials. Andrew is looking into those, as well."

"What about all the arrests he's made?" Keegan's mind swam with the names of all the scoundrels the marshal had collared on their land alone. He waved a hand. "Dale Feather-fall, Garth Swingler, Dalton Gentry, Mortimer Copeland..."

"Yes, he did." Gray's jaw looked like it was set in stone. "And every last one of them was released from jail a couple of months ago. Andrew checked. All on the same night, too. It's the oddest thing."

Keegan was perplexed. "Why would he just up and let 'em go like that?" They were criminals, for crying out loud!

"That's the question of the century," Gray sighed.

By now, Keegan's brothers and Bo had joined them in the front yard.

Bo must have overheard most of what Gray had said,

because he slapped a fist into his palm. "If that doesn't beat all!"

Carlton folded his arms, his dark gaze narrowing on Keegan's. "Clearly, he's been playing a much longer game than we ever gave him credit for."

Redding balled his fists at his sides. "If that reprobate has gone rogue and emptied out the jail, it means both Annabelle and Penelope are in danger again, right alongside the rest of our wives."

Keegan's brain had already gone there. The marshal had clearly changed in the time that they'd known him. It was truly unfortunate. "Since we have no idea how deep his corruption runs, we can't place our trust in anyone we haven't personally vetted going forward," he warned. "We have to assume anyone connected to him might be in on his shenanigans."

"Shenanigans?" Carlton raised his eyebrows. "We've been speculating long enough. Now might be a good time to stop and define exactly what we think we're up against here."

"A very long con, from the looks of it." Keegan spread his hands. "My guess is Cane Fraser is on the front end, herding mail-order brides west from both Atlanta and Savannah. Turner King is on the receiving end — intercepting the thwarted grooms, pretending to arrest them, then recruiting them into heaven-only-knows what!"

Gray gave an irritated jerk of his head back toward the distant mountain range. "We know he's got a brothel where the brides are being held hostage."

"I don't think this so-called brothel is his end game, though." The more Keegan thought about it, the more convinced he was that the corrupt marshal was hunting bigger game like southern family fortunes — a whole bunch of them. "That's why it's in such a remote location. We've been looking at this all wrong. It's possible the brothel is little more than a holding cell for the heiresses whose fortunes they've swindled."

"Why keep them alive at all?" Carlton demanded.

"I reckon it's for the same reason he needed the rejected grooms out of jail." Gray's eyebrows drew together ferociously.

The truth finally sank home for Keegan. "They're going to force the hostages to marry the blokes," he declared gloomily. "At least on paper." It was barbaric and unthinkable, but it was the only thing that connected all the dots.

"I'm afraid so," Gray agreed in austere tones.

Keegan longed to pound his fist into something as he quickly puzzled through the rest of the details. "According to my wife, a lot of those old southern family fortunes are tied up in complicated wills that require them to marry in order to inherit anything."

Gray expelled a heavy breath. "More than likely, the crooked grooms have agreed to sign marriage certificates in exchange for a cut in the loot."

"Money is usually what attracts criminals," Keegan agreed.

"In that case..." Carlton started ticking off a list on his fingers. "We can assume Dale Featherfall is earmarked for Annabelle, Dalton Gentry will be paired with Penelope, and Mark Hudson's imposter has been brought into town because of Eliza Jane. Who do they have lined up for Magnolia, Emmaline, and Olivia Joy?"

"They still have Garth Swingler and Mortimer Copeland waiting on the sidelines," Redding pointed out. "Plus Turner King, himself."

Bo spread his hands. "If they've got all the pieces in place, what are they waiting for?"

Keegan shook his head. He'd been wondering the same thing. "The right time? The right opportunity? It's anyone's guess." The longer Turner King took to make his move, though, the harder it was going to be for him to succeed. The townsfolk of El Vaquero hadn't been sitting around on their hands during the interim. They'd added more than fifty new ranch hands and range riders to their ranks since Christmas day alone.

A rumble of thunder made their heads tip back in unison. Clouds rolled and seethed above them. A flash of lightning flickered over the distant mountain range.

"There's the snow we've been expecting." Normally, Keegan welcomed every season, but he wasn't overly enamored with the greenish-gray cast of the skies this morning. Turner and his gang tended to crawl out of hiding like bugs in the night. If the coming storm made things dark enough, they might decide to make a move against Ford Ranch during daylight hours instead.

As Gray passed biscuits and ham around their circle, Keegan stepped closer to him to be heard above the rumble of thunder. "The marshal might see the incoming snowstorm as an opportunity. We need to put everyone at Ford Ranch on full alert."

"Agreed. We need to keep our patrols running no matter how thick the snow gets."

"Uh, folks?" Bo's words were slurred since he was talking with his mouth full.

Keegan's younger brothers were busy kicking around a pebble between them while they ate, not paying them any mind. However, Keegan and Gray glanced Bo's way and found him pointing toward the mountain range.

Two stooped figures emerged from the nearest pass. They trudged in the direction of the boarding house, moving in an odd zigzagging manner. Were they drunk?

Bo shoved the last half of his biscuit in his mouth and reached for his pair of pistols.

"Heads up!" Keegan barked to alert his younger brothers.

He drew his pistols, craning for a better look at the two figures heading their way. As he watched, one of them stumbled and fell face forward in the snow.

A distinctly female scream followed.

Bo frowned over at Keegan. "Sounds like she's calling for help."

Keegan's jaw tightened. "It could be a trap."

"It could be anything," Bo agreed, "but I'm a minister. I'm going out there. Will you cover me?"

Keegan clenched his teeth. No way was he sending his best friend alone into the jaws of danger. "I'm going with you."

"Wait a blessed second," Carlton growled. "Ya'll aren't expendable. Keegan, you help run the whole shebang at Ford Ranch, and Bo—"

"We'll go." Chevy motioned for Lance to follow him as he strode away from the boarding house. "Y'all got wives to consider. We don't."

Lance trotted to catch up with him.

"Oh, for the love of—!" Keegan flanked right and followed his youngest brothers. He was in no mood for theatrics or heroics. Whatever was happening out there on the snowy field needed to be dealt with before it became a bigger problem.

Bo flanked left, following his lead while Carlton and Redding trailed a short distance behind them with Gray. Every man had his guns drawn. They were prepared for anything.

As they drew closer to the two figures, they found a dark-haired woman sobbing as if her heart would break. She was tugging at the arm of her fallen comrade. "Please get up, Turner," she begged piteously. "They're nearly upon us!"

Turner? Keegan frowned as his gaze fastened on the crumpled black overcoat of the man in the snow. "Did you say Turner, as in Turner King?" He broke into a jog, with both guns aimed at the corrupt marshal.

Glancing in Keegan's direction, the woman visibly wilted.

She raised her hands in the air. "We're unarmed," she cried piteously. The mountain breeze viciously whipped the hair off her forehead, revealing a purplish bruise rising over her right eye.

Keegan reached the man it the black coat and nudged him over with the toe of his boot.

It was, indeed, Turner King — a much thinner, gaunter version of him than the man who'd joined them for breakfast on Christmas morning. His cheeks were so sunken that they were downright skeletal.

"I c-can't get him to w-wake up," the woman quavered in a distinctly southern accent. Despite her bedraggled state, her spine was stiff and her blue gaze defiant as she stared back at Keegan.

"Who are you?" he demanded, shoving his guns back in his holsters. Every instinct in him was shouting that she posed no threat to them.

"M-Meredith Hayes."

He eyed her with concern. She was past the first blush of youth, closer to the marshal's age than his own. However, she'd once been a woman of means. The hem of her gown was edged with thick embroidery that had cost someone a pretty penny to tailor.

"Where are you from?" he pressed, kneeling beside Turner King. He scooped the wasted marshal into his arms and stood with him.

Miss Hayes slowly lowered her arms. "What are you g-going to d-do with him?"

"Turn him over to the sheriff, I reckon." Keegan shook his head at the man in his arms, wondering if the strange tint to his nose was frostbite.

"Please don't do that! You might as well leave him in the snow and let him die."

"Why?" Keegan glared at her as he started to walk back toward the boarding house.

"We don't know who to trust anymore." Her voice was pleading as she stumbled to catch up to him. She tripped on the hem of her dress and would have fallen if Bo's arm hadn't shot out.

He snatched her up like a sack of potatoes and kept walking. He quickly caught up to Keegan. Gray tromped through the snow on the other side of him, while the younger Ford brothers stayed in the rear and kept their weapons at the ready.

"With all due respect, lady, this fellow has been pretending to arrest criminals, then letting them go."

"Not him!" She struggled to sit up straighter in Bo's arms. "He's the real Turner King. A friend of the Fords. We've been walking for hours, trying to make it to their ranch."

"Well, he succeeded."

"You mean you're a Ford?" Cautious hope stained her emaciated features. She wasn't in much better shape than the marshal.

"One of them."

"Thank the good Lord," she breathed. Her eyes filled with tears.

Keegan dropped his gaze. He'd never been able to stomach seeing a woman cry. "So, there's more than one Turner King?" he inquired gruffly. He hadn't seen this coming.

"Of course not!" Meredith Hayes' voice was as tart as a crabapple. "The other one is only pretending to be him. He captured my Turner while he was trying to rescue me and the other mail-order brides."

"Your Turner?" Keegan raised his eyebrows, swiveling his head to catch her eye again.

Her face turned beet red. "The marshal sent off for a mail-order bride of his own," she murmured, brushing at the dampness.

"You." Keegan's lips twitched. It certainly sounded like something a single and lonely marshal might do. It didn't explain why the two men resembled each other, though — so much that it was uncanny. "Why does the other Turner King look so much like this one?"

"They're half brothers," she supplied dully. "Turner was the illegitimate one, of all things, but his father loved him more than his legitimate son. Or so Nathan King claims."

At Keegan's puzzled look, she hastened to explain. "That's the name of the legitimate one. He was furious when his father legally adopted his half brother right before he passed. He tried to fight it in court, but it didn't go anywhere."

"Why fight it at all?" Keegan didn't see any point.

"I don't know." She looked genuinely perplexed. "According to Turner, there wasn't any money to speak of, though Nathan seems to think otherwise. He claims Turner stole their father's fortune. Between you, me, and the doorpost, it wouldn't make a lick of sense to do that right before dedicating himself to a life of selfless service as a U.S. Marshal. Anyone with the sense God gave them knows it's not an easy job." Her blue gaze glowed with admiration. "But that's just how Turner is. Honorable and brave. He loves God, his country...and me," she added shyly.

They reached the construction site and untethered two of the horses. Keegan rode back to Ford Ranch with Turner King draped across the front of his saddle. Bo rode back with Meredith Hayes riding side-saddle in front of him.

Penelope met them at the door of the farmhouse. "What in the world?" Her sleeves were rolled up and her hair was pulled back with a ribbon. It looked as if they'd caught her in the middle of her chores.

"Apparently, this is the real Turner King." Keegan pointed at the man dangling from his saddle. "And this is his mail-order bride, Meredith Hayes." He angled his head toward the woman in Bo's saddle. "She was kidnapped and held hostage during her journey west, he went after her, and got captured himself — by his half-brother, no less, who's been posing as him ever since."

"That's quite a story!" Annabelle's eyes were as wide as saucers and brimming with sympathy as she ushered them into the living room. "He doesn't look so good. Let's get him inside and see what we can do for him."

Turner King was in such bad shape that Keegan feared he might not make it. His pulse was weak and his breathing was labored. However, the womenfolk at Ford Ranch were no strangers to nursing wounded and ill cowboys. They'd do their best by him.

His mother bustled into the living room from the kitchen with the sleeves of her white blouse rolled up like Penelope's. She took one look at the unconscious man in Keegan's arms and instructed him to deposit his burden on the sofa. Then she had him stir the fire and add a few more sticks of wood to get it roaring again.

She sent Penelope across the yard to Annabelle and Ethan's cabin to fetch some bandages and medical supplies. While Penelope was away, she proceeded to strip the marshal down to his waist to examine his wounds more closely. He'd been badly beaten, but the dark spot on his nose turned out to be nothing more than a mixture of dirt and dried blood. It wasn't frostbite after all.

Penelope returned with the required supplies. Annabelle accompanied her, looking even more swollen with child than she had the day before. "I know you're not looking for spectators," she noted wryly, rubbing a hand over her belly, "but I had to see him for myself." She was wearing the same high-waisted gown that her friends always insisted made her look like a Georgia peach.

Catching sight of Turner King on the sofa, she shook her head in amazement. "It's really him, isn't it?"

"It's really him," Keegan affirmed. "We're as flabbergasted as you are."

The three women worked together quickly and efficiently to treat and bandage the marshal's injuries. Then they piled him with clean blankets.

Meredith refused to leave his side the entire time they were tending to him. She kept up a constant trail of conversation that Keegan highly doubted the unconscious man could hear.

"We made it to safety, just like you said we would," she informed him in a tremulous voice. "We're safe now." She brushed his shaggy blonde hair back from his forehead. It was in sore need of a trim. Under Paloma's direction, she also squeezed liquid past his parched lips from a damp cloth.

He lay there unmoving for more than an hour. To her credit, Meredith refused to bathe, eat, or get comfortable. She wept and prayed over him, clinging to his hand.

His eyelids suddenly popped open. He stared blankly at her for the space of a heartbeat. Then his gaunt features relaxed. "It wasn't a dream." His voice was slurred with exhaustion as he squeezed her fingers. "We made it!"

"Yes, sweetheart. We did. The Fords found us and brought us the rest of the way to their home." She leaned over him to brush her lips against his. A fresh round of tears dripped between them, splashing on his cheeks and nose.

He didn't seem to mind. Reaching up to touch her face, he kissed her back. "I'm going to make this right."

"Yes, you are," Bo drawled from the other side of the room. His voice was infused with humor. "From where I'm standing, this lovely lady has been sorely compromised. You'll marry her before the day is through, or my name isn't Reverend Bo Stanley."

Turner King grinned against the lips of his affianced.

"That's the plan, reverend. That's always been the plan." His voice was growing stronger.

Blushing, Meredith lifted her head. "We signed a marriage contract months ago. Most unfortunately, I was intercepted by bandits on my way to Texas. I don't know what would have become of me if Turner hadn't worked so hard to track me down."

"Why didn't you ask for our help?" Keegan glared at the marshal. He couldn't believe the man had foolishly charged into danger without any backup. Then again, he'd never before seen the besotted version of him. Love could do crazy things to a man's sense of reason.

"It's a long story." Turner sounded tired again. "The short version is, even a U.S. Marshal can get in over his head."

"Do you still have your badge?" Keegan's mind raced over everything they'd learned today.

"Is the sky blue?" The marshal's voice was dry.

"Technically, it's green and gray today." As if on cue, another belt of thunder slapped the skies overhead.

"My credentials are intact, though I reckon my higher-ups are going to want an explanation about how my imposter emptied the jail in El Gato." His mouth twisted bitterly. "No doubt my scoundrel of a half brother has been flashing around the gold star he ripped from my uniform."

Keegan was just glad the marshal was still around to set the record straight. "It's good to have you back." He reached over the back of the sofa to clasp the marshal's hand. "Really good." He was less concerned about their coming confrontation with the outlaws now that they had a federal marshal on their side again. A real one.

Eliza Jane flew into the living room a few minutes later. Magnolia, Emmaline, and Olivia Joy were on her heels. "Oh, my lands, Keegan!" She moved across the room to slide her arms around him from behind while the other women ran to check on their own husbands.

Keegan turned his head her way to nuzzle her cheek. She was wearing her hair down the way he preferred it, cascading over the shoulders of her pine green gown. He never grew tired of running his fingers through the silky strands.

She leaned into his kiss, declaring breathlessly, "We saw your horses out front and were worried half to death that something had happened at the boarding house—" She abruptly stopped talking as she caught sight of the marshal on the other side of the sofa.

"Oh, my lands," she breathed again, hugging her husband tighter. "What is he doing here?" Her gaze landed on the young woman kneeling on the floor in front of the sofa. "Who is she?"

Turner King smiled faintly up at her. "I'm U.S. Marshal Turner King, ma'am. The real one, and I'm mighty pleased to meet you."

"The real one!" She gave Keegan an excited shake. "Good gracious, Mr. Ford. Every time I let you out of my sight, trouble finds you."

"I like her." Turner King's smile widened into a grin as he met Keegan's eye.

"So do I." Keegan tugged Eliza Jane around to the other side of the sofa to face the newcomers. "Enough to marry her." He held out her hand so the marshal could see the diamond ring she was wearing.

"Congratulations, my friend!" Turner King shook his head in wonder. "Clearly, I missed a few things while I was away."

"We'll get you caught up," Bo assured in a humorous voice. "Right after we get you married."

The marshal sobered. "You'd best make it quick, reverend,

because Nathan and his men are going to be hot on my trail in nothing flat."

Recalling the absence of a fire on the mountain for the past twelve hours, Keegan's gaze narrowed in consideration on Turner and Meredith. "When did you two escape?"

"Last night, my friend. Only by the grace of God did we make it off the mountain alive." Turner regretfully shared the news that there were still two other mail-order brides in his half brother's clutches. "We have to go after them."

"We will." Keegan gave an up-down nod. "Your escape must be why Nathan and his goons weren't spying on us for once. They were too busy searching for you."

Another clap of thunder shook the room. Then another. It sounded like it was moving closer.

"That was more than thunder, folks." Bo's voice held a note of warning.

"What do you mean?" Annabelle asked worriedly, glancing toward the sound.

A volley of shots followed, answering the question before Bo could. Some sounded far away, others at closer range.

"It sounds like our range riders are firing back," Keegan announced tersely. The gunfire rapidly increased in intensity, like a bowl of popcorn erupting over an open fire.

Ford Ranch was under attack!

Chapter 10: Icy Encounter

ELIZA JANE

"No rest for the weary!" With a grunt of pain, Turner King struggled to sit up on the sofa. The pile of quilts slid from his shoulders and bunched around his waist.

His fiancée gave a low cry of protest and tried to coax him back into a horizontal position. "Sweetheart, you can't—"

He stubbornly remained upright, glancing around the room as if searching for something. "Bo, you've got to marry us." His gaze latched on to the mountain man. "Now!"

Bo glanced their way in amazement. "We're a little busy here, marshal."

The Ford brothers were rushing around the farmhouse, pulling out rifles and a stockpile of ammunition. Bo was sliding a china cabinet across the nearest window, while Chevy and Lance wedged a chair beneath the handle of the front door.

"Just say the words, my friend, and keep it quick," the marshal urged. "It's the best way I can protect Meredith in my current state."

"You want the quick version, eh?" Bo's bushy eyebrows rose.

"If they catch up to us, they're going to force her to marry one of those blasted—"

"U.S. Marshal Turner King," Bo boomed without any more preamble, "do you take this woman to be your wife, to have and to hold from this day forward, for better, for worse, for richer, for poorer, in sickness and in health, to love and to cherish, until death do you part?"

"Yes, I do!" The marshal's tawny gaze burned into Meredith's.

Eliza Jane's heart tugged with a mixture of admiration and sympathy for the bedraggled couple. They'd been through so much in recent weeks. They were filthy, exhausted, and caught in the middle of a firefight. Most importantly, though, they were in love — undeniably so.

"Meredith Hayes," Bo's gaze dropped to the woman who remained on her knees beside the sofa, "do you take this man to be your husband, to have and to hold from this day forward, for better, for worse, for richer, for poorer, in sickness and in health, to love and to cherish, until death do you part?"

"I do." Her voice was choked with emotion. She clung to the marshal's hand like it was a lifeline.

Eliza Jane imagined that he'd rescued her from both her captivity and a life of spinsterhood.

"By the power vested in me by the State of Texas, I pronounce you husband and wife." Bo never stopped working the whole time he was officiating their rapid-fire wedding ceremony.

"Thank you, reverend." Despite the direness of their present circumstances, Turner King couldn't seem to tear his gaze away from his new bride.

Bo tossed a grin their way. "I'll write up your marriage certificate when I get back to the church. Let me know who you want to sign as witnesses. You've got a whole pile of them to choose from."

"We really appreciate this." Meredith's gaze sparkled with happiness. She'd gotten married without flowers, music, or even a church building, but there wasn't so much as a hint of regret in her voice or expression.

"You'll have to celebrate later." Keegan's voice was apologetic as he lifted weapons from their stockpile and started tossing them to people around the room.

Eliza Jane caught her lower lip between her teeth when he lobbed a rifle — barrel facing up — toward the sofa.

After only the faintest hesitation, Meredith's slender hand shot out and closed around it.

"Nice catch!" Eliza Jane gave her an admiring nod. "Do you know how to shoot?"

"Better than most. My pa made sure of it," the woman affirmed dryly. "He always wanted a son, but he got me instead."

Eliza Jane sympathized with what the bride had left unsaid. Apparently, her pa had trusted her with everything besides their family fortune, and this was where it had gotten her — in the crosshairs of an unscrupulous criminal gang. Then again, it had also caused her path to cross with that of Turner King.

Unfortunately, their troubles were far from over yet.

"Darlin'?" Keegan's voice reclaimed Eliza Jane's attention.

She hurried to his side to accept the handgun he had outstretched. It wasn't from the stockpile near the fireplace. She'd watched him pull it from the back waistband of his denim trousers.

"This is like the one you were carrying the day you arrived in town." He quickly demonstrated how to fire and reload it.

"You don't need to worry about me." She lifted her chin. "I'll do my part."

"I'm sorry it's come to this." His dark eyes raked over her

features, silently begging for her forgiveness. "All I ever wanted was to keep you safe."

"Well, I'm not sorry." She accepted the weapon and held it pointed down at the floor. "I'm tired of ducking, running, and losing ground. For once, I'm going to get to fight back. It feels good, Keegan. If that makes me a bad person, I'm sorry."

Smirking, he reached out to tweak her nose. "I believe what it makes you is a complete hoyden."

"I tried to warn you," she reminded softly.

"That you did." The look he gave her indicated that he very much planned to demonstrate what he thought of his hoyden wife...later.

Keegan and Bo used a mix of commands and hand signals to get everyone in position around the farmhouse. They took their places at the living room and dining room windows in the front of the house, as well as the parlor and bedroom windows in the back. Chevy and Lance volunteered to man the lookout positions on the floor above them, providing two additional marksmen at the second-story windows.

Keegan moved to one of the living room windows and motioned for Eliza Jane to stand on the opposite side of it. "The fighting might not reach us," he called to anyone who was listening. "Arming up like this is only a precaution. Ethan and our range riders are out there right now, putting it all on the line for us. He's been patrolling ranches and herds his entire life, so you can rest assured he's prepared for this."

At the mention of Ethan's name, Eliza Jane's gaze sought out his wife to make sure she was doing alright. She found Annabelle sagging against the wall beside the front door. She was clutching a pistol in one hand and her belly in the other hand. Without warning, her head jerked back against the wall. She clenched her teeth to hold back a scream.

"Annabelle!" Eliza Jane sprinted across the room in her friend's direction, nearly tripping on the hem of her new gown. *Good gracious!* Not for the first time, she wished she had on a pair of trousers. Being a woman had its clear challenges, not the least of which was unexpectedly going into labor.

She tucked her handgun into the sash at her side as she reached the expectant mother. "It's the baby, isn't it?"

Annabelle gulped, looking terrified. "He's not due to arrive for another month."

Using the pads of her fingers, Eliza Jane gently examined her friend's midsection and determined the babe's head was facing down. That was good. To her chagrin, she additionally noted a pool of dampness on the floor between Annabelle's shoes.

Oh, dear! "My sweet friend," she crooned, trying to swallow the alarm rising in her own throat. "I don't think we get to decide when it's time for a baby to make an appearance. The good Lord does."

"Indeed, He does." Paloma joined them at the door and placed one of Annabelle's arms around her neck for support. She nodded at Eliza Jane to do the same. "You've earned yourself a little resting time, my dear."

She led them to the dining room table. While they balanced Annabelle between them, she raised her voice and hollered, "Meredith, bring me some of those blankets from the sofa!"

Meredith joined them only moments later. Quickly sizing up the situation, she mechanically started laying out blankets on the table. "Up you go," she urged, helping Paloma and Eliza Jane lift Annabelle onto them.

"Since you know where everything is, go boil some water," Paloma instructed Eliza Jane.

"That's alright. I'll handle it." Penelope abandoned her post by one of the windows to dash into the kitchen.

Eliza Jane was grateful for the extra help. She didn't like the idea of leaving Annabelle's side.

"What's going on in there?" Keegan's voice sounded strained from the living room.

Eliza Jane popped her head around the doorway. "Baby's on the way." She shook her head at him. "Don't worry. Your hoyden remains armed and ready, come what may."

He nodded, but there was no answering smirk this time. He wasn't anymore thrilled than she was at the thought of delivering a babe in the middle of a gunfight.

"We've got this," she assured him quietly. "Just keep the wolves outside for us."

He nodded and pointed upward. "From your mouth to God's ears, darlin'." Then he returned his attention to what was happening outside the window.

Paloma rolled up a linen napkin and had Annabelle bite down on it. "Don't you worry about what's happening out there," she instructed firmly. "The others will protect us. You just focus all your energy on bringing my first grandchild into the world, you hear?"

Annabelle nodded so fiercely that a few tears shook loose from the corners of her eyes. They trickled down the sides of her face.

Eliza Jane had heard someone say that Paloma considered Ethan Vasquez to be her seventh son. From the way she was acting, Eliza Jane knew it must be true.

With the skill of a midwife, she calmly talked Annabelle through her breathing and pushing, all the while never ceasing her instruction to everyone else around her.

"Hold her hand to give her something else to squeeze while she's pushing," she ordered Eliza Jane.

During the next push, Annabelle threw her head back and moaned loudly around the cloth in her mouth. More tears slid from the corners of her eyes.

Paloma folded back her skirts. "He's coming," she announced excitedly.

Eliza Jane's eyes filled with tears of apprehension. It felt like everything was happening too fast. Was it normal? Was Annabelle going to be alright? Was the babe going to survive coming so early?

More gunfire popped in the distance. The winds were picking up and wailing on the other side of the windows, rattling the panes. The plink of hail mixed with snow sounded against the glass.

Eliza watched her friend on the table bear down and push yet again. This time, the cloth fell from her mouth, and her scream filled the room.

Eliza Jane had never felt so helpless. So desperate. So out of options. Her lips parted, and she started to pray.

"Please, God, be in the room with us. Keep Annabelle strong and give her a healthy baby. Protect every man and woman on Ford Ranch right now. You are the Keeper of the storm raging outside. You are our safe haven in the middle of our troubles."

In the other room, she heard Bo join in the prayer. He asked for protection over the ranch hands, range riders, cowboys, and their wives. A sense of peace stole over her as his deep voice boomed alongside hers. She ended her prayer with a simple statement of gratitude.

"Your grace is sufficient for today and every day, Lord. Amen."

"Amen," Paloma, Meredith, and Olivia Joy echoed.

"Amen!" Bo bellowed from the other side of the house.

A new cry pierced the room. Annabelle's baby had finally made his appearance.

He was a tiny, red-faced lad — a bit smaller than most babies, probably because he was a month early. Despite his size, he came out kicking his legs and waving his fists like an energetic kitten.

Annabelle's tear drenched gaze followed him longingly as

Paloma lifted him for her to see. "My precious son," she crooned, leaning weakly back on her elbows.

The toughest part was over, and she was going to be alright. Eliza Jane could see it in her friend's eyes.

"My grandson is a fighter!" Paloma's dark eyes glistened with tears of joy as she quickly washed the babe and clipped his cord. Swaddling him in a fresh towel, she handed him over to his mama.

Eliza Jane ducked her head around the dining room wall again to deliver a happy smile to her husband. She knew he was anxiously waiting for an update.

He nodded, his dark eyes turning a tad glassy with relief.

"Ethan and I talked about names," Annabelle panted as she guided the babe's head to latch on and start nursing. "In the end, we decided to keep it simple and name him after his daddy."

"You knew it was going to be a son?" Eliza Jane was thoroughly mystified. She moved back to her friend's side. "How?"

"I don't know. I just did." Annabelle gave a breathy chuckle.

"Well, you were right. Little Ethan is beautiful," Eliza Jane sighed. She'd been around babies before, but she couldn't remember ever feeling so attached to one like this. Having one of her dearest friends in the world become a mother was so much more personal. She felt a little like the babe belonged to her, too.

"Ethan James Vasquez II," Annabelle declared happily. "We're going to call him Jimmy so we don't have two people forever trying to answer to the same name at the same time."

"Little Jimmy," Eliza Jane repeated. It suited him. When Annabelle finished nursing him, she held out her arms. "May I?"

"Of course!" Annabelle's tear-drenched face glowed with pride and pleasure as she handed him over. "I want him to meet all of his aunties right away." At Eliza Jane's surprised look, she chuckled. "Oh, come on! We're practically sisters. What else would he call you?" She pointed in delight at each of them. "Aunt Eliza Jane. Aunt Olivia Joy." Her gaze landed on Paloma next. "And Grandma."

"His *abuela*." Their mother-in-law briefly lapsed into her native tongue. "I've actually always fancied being called Nana."

"Oh, how sweet!" Annabelle looked charmed. "It'll certainly be easier for him to say."

Eliza Jane sashayed a few steps toward the doorway with little Jimmy. In a burst of inspiration, she danced with him all the way into the hall to show him off to everyone else.

Keegan's gaze softened with wonder at the sight of them. *I love you,* he mouthed.

I love you, too, she mouthed back.

As she smiled dreamily at him, it slowly dawned on her that she could no longer hear any gunfire. She grew still and listened.

"It's over, folks." Reverend Bo Stanley lowered his gun. "It appears the Lord has seen fit to answer our prayers."

In less than a minute, a knock sounded on the front door of the farmhouse. "It's me. Ethan," their senior range rider called in an urgent voice.

Keegan lunged across the room to remove the chair from beneath the door handle. He unlocked the door and cautiously cracked it open. Then he pushed it wider.

Ethan stomped the snow from his boots and slapped his Stetson against the outside wall before stepping inside.

"Congratulations!" Keegan threw his arms around him and gave him a joyful pounding between the shoulder blades.

"Eh...you're welcome." Ethan looked surprised, though he slapped his friend's shoulders in return before stepping back. "It wasn't much of a fight, to be honest. They came out guns a-blazing. Then it started to sleet and hail like I've never seen before. Their side got the worst of it. Fist sized pieces that knocked every last one of them out cold. It was nothing short of a miracle."

Bo ambled across the living room to join them in the foyer. "He who dwells in the shelter of the Most High will abide in the shadow of the Almighty." His grin was exultant. "It's one of my favorite Psalms."

Ethan nodded wryly. "That's better than any explanation I can come up with for what happened out there."

"What's the status of our folks?" Keegan inquired quickly.

"Everyone is accounted for. No casualties. Only one injury that we know of. One of our newest range riders got grazed by a bullet. Jameson is patching up his arm as we speak."

"And the outlaws?"

"Tied up like Christmas geese, every one of them. Just need to figure out who we can trust to make the arrests." Ethan scanned the room. His gaze darkened at the sight of Turner King lounging on the sofa. "What in the blazes?" His hand went to his holster.

"He's the real Turner King!" Eliza Jane moved to the rear of their huddle, lightly bouncing on the balls of her feet to keep little Jimmy quiet. She couldn't wait to reveal his presence to his daddy.

Keegan gave an exaggerated sweep of his arm toward the sofa. "Our marshal and his beloved mail-order bride were captured by his half brother a few months ago. The scoundrel swiped his badge and has been posing as a U.S. Marshal ever since."

"Surely you jest!" Ethan couldn't have looked more astounded. He moved into the living room to take a closer look at the marshal. After a moment, his expression cleared. "You went and got yourself married, eh?" He thrust out a hand. "You sly dog, you!"

Turner weakly clasped it. "Actually, Bo did the honors just this afternoon. We weren't sure how this firefight would end. Giving Meredith my name added one more layer of protection between her and what those scoundrels had planned for her." He swung his legs over the side of the sofa. "Speaking of what they've been planning, there are two more mail-order brides in need of rescuing from the mountains. Has anyone gone after them yet?"

Ethan held up a hand to stop him. "How about you just tell us their whereabouts and sit this one out?"

"Gladly." Turner looked relieved. "Congratulations, by the way."

"Thanks, I reckon." Ethan looked puzzled all over again. "Not sure why y'all keep lathering it on so thick, though. I was only doing my job, the same as you."

"Because you're a father now." Eliza Jane moved over to the sofa so he could see the babe in her arms. Little Jimmy was sucking contentedly on two tiny fingers. His eyelids were drooping sleepily.

Ethan took a hitching step in her direction. Then another. "Where's Annabelle?" His face paled. "Is she—?"

"She's fine. Go see for yourself." Eliza Jane nodded toward the dining room. "Here. Take this sweet bundle with you." She ever so gently deposited his newborn son in his arms.

Ethan gazed in wonder down at the miniature version of himself. "My son," he whispered. Then he strode with the babe into the dining room.

"Isn't he precious?" Eliza Jane threw her arms excitedly around Keegan. "Oh, my lands, Keegan! He has the tiniest ten fingers, the tiniest ten toes, and the most beautiful blue eyes. He's perfect!"

His chuckle sounded a little hoarse as he hugged her back. "Almost makes a fellow want to have a little hoyden of his own someday." Ducking his head to speak against her ear, he added. "Or two. Or three."

"So, you're ready to start a family?" she whispered back.

"I am." He nuzzled his way across her cheek to the edge of her mouth. "All in God's timing, of course."

"Me, too." She was thrilled to learn that they wanted the same thing. "I want as many hoydens as He sees fit to give us."

"Yes, please." Ignoring the fact that they had an audience, Keegan tipped her face up to his for the tenderest of kisses.

Epilogue

Two years later

Eliza Jane couldn't believe how quickly El Vaquero had grown since her first Christmas there. Though no one had struck gold, the locals kept referring to it as a boomtown.

Main Street was now crammed end-to-end with businesses. Bo and Olivia Joy's church greeted all newcomers at the beginning of the street, and the lovely adobe Ford House welcomed them to stay a night at the end of the street. She and Keegan lived in an adjoining apartment, just like they'd always planned to. A year ago, their first little hoyden, Keegan Michael Ford, had made his appearance.

Eliza Jane smiled as she leaned across the railing on the front porch with her cup of tea cupped between her hands. It was a cold January morning, but she preferred watching the sunrise in person instead of simply staring at it through the window.

A muffled, boyish chortle alerted her to the fact that little Michael was finally awake. She didn't immediately return indoors, knowing Keegan would look after him for a bit.

Taking another sip of her tea, she waited until the sun was blasting over the horizon before turning around and tugging her cloak more tightly around her throat.

She let herself noiselessly back inside so as not to disturb the guests who were still sleeping. Tiptoeing down the hallway, she made her way to the back parlor where she, Keegan, and Michael enjoyed their private family time.

Little Michael toddled across the room, dragging a toy dog on a string. His father had purchased it at the General Store down the street.

"Woof! Woof!" he cried excitedly, dragging the toy in a circle around the pianoforte.

Eliza Jane shushed him with a finger against her lips. "You never slow down, do you, little tiger?" She'd seriously never encountered another human being with so much energy. He woke up with a shout every morning and hit the floor running. He didn't slow down until his nap time. Sometimes, he played so hard leading up to it that he fell asleep in mid-sentence, leaning against a chair. He was truly entertaining to watch.

"I warned you we should get the little hoyden a real dog and be done with it." Keegan towered over their son, keeping a close eye on him. To give Eliza Jane a break, he started nearly every morning with an hour of father-son time. Afterward, he made his way to Ford Ranch, where he still served as ranch manager.

Jameson, who'd formerly shared the position with him, had been elected the first mayor of El Vaquero. His wife was in heaven serving as the town's first lady. She'd put every one of her southern belle skills to good use, hosting the most wonderful dinner parties, fundraisers, and holiday celebrations at Town Hall.

"A dog? Do you really think a dog would bring less noise into the lives of our guests?" Eliza Jane took a seat on the blue upholstered divan, fluffing her winter gold skirt around her ankles. Leaning back, she took another contented sip of her tea.

"Not at all, darlin'." Keegan bent over her to plant a slow, tender kiss on her lips. "It would, however, give Michael something to chase. A frisky little pup with the energy to match his own."

"Does such a creature even exist?" She chuckled merrily. "I've yet to meet another person, old or young, with half his energy."

Keegan perched on the edge of the divan and winked at her. "I reckon that's what happens when you match a cowboy with a hoyden."

As she smiled at his words, her breathing turned shallow. The sight of him in his leather vest and white button-up shirt never failed to take her breath away. She adored every inch of him, from the tiny laugh lines at the edges of his eyes, to his square bronze chin, to the hint of an evening shadow that showed up only minutes after he shaved each morning.

"Do you like what you see, Mrs. Ford?" He waggled his dark eyebrows at her.

"Are you fishing for compliments again, Mr. Ford?"

"I could fish," he drawled slowly, "but I'd much rather do this." He reached for her cup of tea and set it on the windowsill behind her. Then he reached for her hands and used them to tug her into his arms.

"You're supposed to be watching Michael," she murmured between kisses.

"I can do both this and that."

"Can you?" she taunted, drawing his head down for another kiss. "Because it's gotten really quiet, don't you think? Too quiet, Mr. Ford."

"You might have a point, Mrs. Ford." With a resigned

expulsion, he gazed around the room to locate the quiet little lad in question.

They found their son removing books from the bookshelf two at a time. He was stacking them on the floor as fast as he could. They watched in fascination as a pen for his toy dog slowly took shape.

Eliza Jane tipped her head against her husband's shoulder. "I think this is the quietest he's ever been," she whispered.

Without warning, little Michael reached for a book on a higher shelf.

"Oh, sweetie, no!" Eliza Jane straightened, but there wasn't enough time to leap up and run across the room. She was forced to watch in frozen silence while the stack of books above his head tumbled down on top of him. One grazed his temple.

He stumbled back with a look of surprise, tripped over the wall of books at his feet, and fell on his backside. His mouth opened in shock, but no sound came out at first. Then he started wailing with gusto.

"Hush, sweetie," Eliza Jane admonished in a stage whisper. *Good gracious!* They had a boarding house full of guests. She looked helplessly at Keegan, begging him to do something.

He snatched up the small boy, twirled him a few times, and pretended to fly him around the room like an insect. He made a humorous buzzing sound while he did it. In no time, Michael forgot his injury and was soon gurgling with laughter again. It wasn't the peace and quiet Eliza Jane longed to give their guests, but it was a lot nicer sound than childish wailing.

She reached for her tea again, content that the first crisis of her day had been averted. Gazing out the bay window, she caught the tiniest glimpse of the back of Magnolia and Emma-line's new theater. With the crooked Cane Fraser and Nathan King behind bars, along with their many partners in crime, the family fortunes of Eliza Jane and her friends had been restored at long last. They were celebrating by living out their dreams at both Ford Ranch and on Main Street.

Olivia Joy still helped out at the boarding house, but she was also painting again. They'd worked out an agreement with her to display her lovely artwork in the living room and dining room at Ford House. She'd sold over a dozen prints already.

Annabelle kept their friends supplied with her ever-growing repertoire of lotions, soaps, and perfumes. They'd erected a display case in front of the check-in booth at Ford House to market her wares. Her products practically flew off the shelves.

For the safety and security of their brides, none of the men at Ford Ranch advertised the fact that they'd married wealthy women. They didn't flaunt it or live any differently than they had before. Behind the scenes, however, they were constantly showering the townsfolk with their generosity. A very prosperous town had blossomed beneath their kindness.

Not wanting to miss out on the exciting new developments happening daily in El Vaquero, U.S. Marshal Turner King had traded in his federal badge to become their local sheriff.

The Fords and their friends had truly done the unthinkable! They'd settled their very own mountain town and grown it into a cattle trading center than rivaled the biggest ranches in Texas.

"You did it!" Eliza Jane turned away from the window with a full heart. There was no other place in the country she'd rather live and raise their son than El Vaquero.

Her husband shot her a questioning look. "Now what have I done?" he teased, flying their son past her.

Michael couldn't stop giggling. "More!" he cried when his father started to slow down.

"You and your brothers built a whole new town. You've

done everything you ever dreamed of." *And I am honored to be a part of it.*

"We built it," he corrected. "My brothers and I couldn't have done even half of this without Bo, Ethan, my mother, Gray, Andrew, and Turner. Not to mention all the skills and talents of our favorite southern belles."

"We do make a great team, don't we?" She beamed a happy smile at him and little Michael.

"The very best," he agreed, "despite my mother's interference." He and his brothers still teased her about her secret role in The Western Moon Agency. Privately, of course, since she'd never gotten around to dissolving the firm. Under Andrew Emerson Esquire's discreet administration, mail-order brides continued to trickle into their remote mountain community.

"Give my love to my favorite mother-in-law when you see her today." Eliza Jane finished her tea, a little sad that their morning hour of family time was coming to an end. "Remind her that she's overdue for a visit, please." Paloma had missed the last one due to helping Penelope with her twin baby girls so she could spend the afternoon decorating for yet another dinner party.

"Oh!" Keegan abruptly set Michael back on his feet, snapping his fingers above the boy's head. "I was supposed to tell you she rescheduled her visit for today."

"Really? What time?" Eliza Jane watched their son go back to building his dog pen, knowing he would be delighted to visit with his Nana. She always brought him homemade cookies and told him the silliest, most engrossing stories.

"Now, I think."

The bell on the front door jingled, and Paloma sailed down the hallway with her arms outstretched. Her brightly embroidered skirts flapped at her ankles like the plume of an exotic bird.

"Where's my favorite Michael?" she called softly.

"Nana!" Michael took a running leap and launched himself into her embrace.

Keegan took advantage of their son's momentary distraction to give his wife a goodbye kiss. "Don't let him grow up too fast while I'm away." He cradled her face between his large hands. "I miss enough as it is."

"Is that your way of saying you want another one?" she teased, kissing him back.

"Yes." He deepened their next kiss. "All in God's timing," he added as he raised his head. It was with great reluctance that he headed for the livery to saddle up for his short ride to Ford Ranch.

All in God's timing. Eliza Jane echoed her husband's words inside her head as she moved to the window to watch the morning brighten a little more. The sun glinted across the soft blanket of snow from the night before. It had yet to be disturbed by very many footprints or wagon wheels. That would change when the town finished waking up.

Everywhere she looked was filled with the beauty of a Master Painter — the white-capped brown and green smudges of the distant mountains, the rippling blue of the western sky, and the spidery branches of bare trees that would be full of blooms again.

Soon.

All in God's timing, just like Keegan always said. She wouldn't have it any other way, because His timing was perfect.

Every time.

Forever and always.

———

Thank you for reading Eliza Jane!
Please leave a review.

MAIL ORDER BRIDES ON THE RUN

A complete trilogy — have you read them all?
Cowboy for Annabelle
Cowboy for Penelope
Cowboy for Eliza Jane

Can't get enough
sweet southern belle romance?
Check out
Elizabeth.
Book #1 in my
Mail Order Brides of Cowboy Creek Series.
An impoverished debutante, a very lonely soldier recently
returned from war, a handful of delightfully interfering
friends, and a mail order bride contract that must be honored
by Christmas...

Happy reading!
Jovie

Sneak Preview: Elizabeth

A lonely soldier, a few interfering friends, and the mail-order bride contract they coax him into signing — just in time for Christmas!

Elizabeth Byrd's friends beg her to join them in Cowboy Creek as a mail-order bride. At first, the former battlefield nurse is scandalized by the idea of marrying a man she's never met, but the war has taken everything from her — her brothers, too many friends to count, and her fiancé. There's nothing left for her in Atlanta but more heartache.

Seeking peace and solitude, Captain David Pemberton retreats to his hunting lodge in Texas the moment the war is over. However, the ranchers in Cowboy Creek don't see fit to leave a widowed soldier alone during Christmas. Insisting he's grieved long enough, they dare him to join them on a holiday venture to acquire wives for them all — a dare he accepts in a weak moment.

He never dreamed he'd recognize the woman who steps off the stagecoach to claim his hand in marriage.

Elizabeth

Available in eBook, paperback, and Kindle Unlimited on Amazon.

MAIL ORDER BRIDES OF COWBOY CREEK

Complete trilogy — read them all!

Elizabeth

Grace

Lilly

Get A Free Book!

Join my mailing list to be the first to know about new releases, free books, special discount prices, Bonus Content, and giveaways.

https://BookHip.com/LSPKMHZ

Note From Jovie

Guess what? There's one more adventure happening in the lives of the swoon-worthy cowboys of El Vaquero.

Because...*drum roll*...I've written one last Bonus Content to celebrate this trilogy. This is something I do exclusively for my for newsletter subscribers, so be sure to sign up for my mailing list.

There's a special Bonus Content chapter for each new book I write (for both my Jovie Grace historicals and Jo Grafford contemporaries). Plus, all my subscribers get a FREE book just for signing up. Woohoo!

Thank you to the moon and back for reading and loving my books.

Jovie

Join Cuppa Jo Readers!

If you're on Facebook, you're invited to join my group, Cuppa Jo Readers. Saddle up for some fun reader games and giveaways + book chats about my sweet and swoon-worthy cowboy book heroes!

https://www.facebook.com/groups/CuppaJoReaders

Sneak Preview: Hot-Tempered Hannah

Unlike his name suggested, there was nothing angelic about Gabriel Donovan. Quite the contrary. While most men were settled down with a wife and family by his ripe old age of twenty-six, he preferred the life of a bounty hunter, tracking and rounding up men who carried a price on their heads. He extracted money and information and taught an occasional lesson to particularly deserving scoundrels when circumstances warranted it.

Most people kept their distance from him, and he was okay with that. More than okay. Making friends wasn't part of the job, and he sincerely hoped he didn't run into anyone he knew at the Pink Swan tonight. Unlike the other patrons, he wasn't looking for entertainment to brighten the endless drag of mining activities in windy Headstone, Arizona. If any of the show girls from the makeshift stage at the front of the room bothered to approach him, they'd be wasting their time. He'd purposefully chosen the dim corner table for its solitude. All he wanted was a hot meal and his own thoughts for company.

"Why, if it isn't Gunslinger Gabe," a female voice cooed,

sweet as honey and smoother than a calf's hide. She plopped a mug of watered down ale on the table, scrapping the metal cup in his direction. "I's beginning to worry you wasn't gonna show up for your Friday night supper."

"Evening, Layla." He hated her use of his nickname. Hated how the printed gazettes popping up across the West ensured he would never outride the cheeky title. It followed him from town to town like an infection. He hated it for one reason: None of his eight notorious years of quick draws and crack shots had been enough to save his partner during that fated summer night's raid.

It was a regret that weighed down his chest every second of every day like a ton of coal. It was a regret he would carry to his grave.

He nodded at the waitress who leaned one hand on the small round table with chipped black paint.

"Well, what's it going to be this time, cowboy?" Her dark eyes snapped with a mixture of interest and impatience. "Bean stew? Mutton pie? As purty as your eyes are, I got other tables to wait on, you know."

The compliment never failed to disgust him. Along with his angelic name, he'd been told more times than he cared to count that he'd been gifted with innocent features. If he heard another word about his clear, lake-blue eyes that inspired trust, he would surely vomit.

"Surprise me." He hoped to change the subject. Both entrees sounded equally good to him. He was hungry enough to eat the pewter serving ware, if she didn't hurry up with his order.

Layla's movements were slow as sap rolling down the bark of a maple tree. "If it's a surprise you're looking for...." She swayed a step closer.

"Bring me both," he said quickly. "The stew and the pie. I haven't eaten since this morning."

"Fine." The single word was infused with a world of derisive disappointment. A few steps into her stormy retreat, she spun around. Anger rippled in waves across her heart-shaped face. "I know what you really want."

"You do?" The question grated out past his lips before he could recall the words. Sarcastic and challenging. It had been a rough day. The last thing he needed was a saloon wench to whip out her crystal ball and presume to know anything about his life. Or his longings. No one this side of the grave could fill the void in his heart.

"I sure do, cowboy." She was back in front of him before he could blink, her scarlet dress shimmering with her movements. "An' I can show you a real special time. Something you ain't never gonna find on no supper menu."

He didn't figure any good would come of trying to explain that his heart belonged to a ghost. Wracking his brain for a sensible way to end their conversation without offending her further, he stared drearily at his mug. There was no quickening of his breathing around any women these days. No increased thump of his heartbeat. Not like there had been with Hannah. His dead partner. Or Hot-Tempered Hannah, as she'd been known throughout the West.

Then again, maybe he wasn't completely dead yet on the inside. He felt a stirring in the sooty, blackened, charred recesses of his brain as his memories of her sprang back to life. Memories that refused to die.

His mind swiftly conjured up all five feet three inches of her boyishly slender frame stuffed in men's breeches along with the tumultuous swing of red hair she'd refused to pin up like a proper lady. Nor could he forget the taunting tilt of her head and the voice that turned from sweet to sassy in a heartbeat, a voice that had been silenced forever due to his failure to reach their rendezvous in time.

Lord help him, but he was finally feeling something alright

— a sharp gushing hole of pain straight through the chest. He mechanically reached for his glass and downed the rest of his ale in one harsh gulp.

"Well, I'll be!" The waitress peered closer at him, at first with amazement then with growing irritation. "I've been around long enough to know when a body's pining for someone else."

What? Am I that transparent? His brows shot up and he stared back, thoroughly annoyed at her intrusive badgering.

Layla was the first to lower her eyes. "Guess I'll get back to work, since you're of no mind to chat." Her frustration raised her voice to a higher pitch. "I was jes' trying to be friendly, you unsociable cad. I'll try not to burn your pie or spill your soup, since that's all you be wanting." Her voice scorched his ears as she pivoted in a full circle and stormed in the direction of the kitchen.

He stared after her, wishing he could call her back but knowing his apology wouldn't make her feel any better. A woman scorned was a deadly thing indeed. He could only hope she didn't poison his supper.

He hunched his shoulders over his corner table and went back to reminiscing about his dead partner. Known as Hot-Tempered Hannah throughout Arizona, she'd stolen his heart with a single kiss then threatened to shoot him if he ever tried to steal another.

He had yet to get over her. Hadn't looked at another woman since. She was three months in the grave, and he was nowhere near moving on with his life.

Layla stomped back in his direction twice. Once to refill his mug and several minutes later to dump his tray on the table with such a clatter that a few droplets of stew spilled over the edge of the bowl.

"A man at one of the faro tables paid me to deliver you a message," she snapped. "He wants you to stick around 'til he's finished dealing. Says he needs to speak with you 'bout somethin' important."

The drowsy contentedness settling in Gabe's bones from the hot meal sharpened back to full awareness. He paused in the act of lifting a spoonful of stew to his mouth. "Which man?"

She pointed to the nearest gaming table. "Over there. The one dealing."

Technically, the man was shuffling, but he pushed back his Stetson an inch and deliberately nodded a greeting in response to their curious stares. Gabe didn't recognize him. They were dressed much the same, albeit Gabe hadn't bothered to remove his trench coat like the other man had.

His keen bounty hunter eyes zeroed in on the ridge of concealed weapons beneath the man's vest. Most people wouldn't have noticed, but Gabe wasn't most people. He was well paid to notice everything around him. The things people wanted him to notice and the things they preferred he didn't.

Those same sensory nodes told him Layla was still present, though she was standing behind him not making a peep. His gaze remained fixed on his summoner. "Does this faro dealer have a name?"

She sniffed. "He didn't say, and I ain't takin' extra to find out. He's working a little too hard for my tastes to fit in, if you know what I mean."

Gabe knew exactly what she meant and was surprised enough at her perception to spare her a glance. He reached in his pocket, and she tensed. He slid an extra bill in her direction across the scratched up tabletop. Something told him she could use the money. "Thanks for passing on the gentleman's message."

The frown on her lacquered lips eased. "Maybe some time you and I can visit a little longer, gunslinger?" She batted her lashes at him.

He highly doubted it — ever. "Dinner tastes wonderful. I thank you for that as well." He returned his hand to his soup spoon and his attention to the faro dealer. Something told him he was about to receive a new bounty assignment.

Layla lingered a few moments longer but finally left him on a drawn-out sigh of resignation.

He ate quickly while observing the card game. In seconds, he determined the game was rigged. Unlike most tables where the odds generally leaned in the banker's favor, this table broke even every few rounds. The intervals were entirely too regular to be coincidental. If Gabe's suspicions were correct, the faro dealer wasn't making a penny. *Very odd.* He chewed his mutton pie more slowly, watching the man.

When the man looked up between rounds, he allowed their gazes to clash once more. A nod from him had a new faro dealer rushing forward to claim the oval table with its green baize covering. The man closed down his rigged game, tucked his crooked gaming box beneath his arm, and sauntered in Gabe's direction amidst the cries for higher stakes from the newest dealer on the floor.

Gabe took in the man's tousled brown hair, even stride, and confident air. His senses told him the man was on a mission but not out for blood. Nevertheless, he kept a hand on his holster as the man stopped beside his table.

"May I join you?" The thick northeastern accent tickled his curiosity further.

A Bostonian, if Gabe was a betting man. Which he wasn't where money was concerned. He dipped his head in agreement without breaking eye contact.

The man took a seat, cradling the card box between his hands on the table in front of him. He was far more at ease than most men tended to be in the presence of Gunslinger Gabe. His long fingers were scarred on one hand, puckered and mottled a permanent shade of salmon as if he'd held his hand in a fire a few moments too long.

"I need your help." His words were simple and quietly spoken, not the usual hard-nosed beginning to a proper bounty negotiation. His tone was missing the sharp bite of revenge or the frantic pace of a man in a hurry.

Gabe leaned forward. "Most reputable men introduce themselves."

A half-grin softened the man's features another degree as he signaled Layla. "Most reputable men are fools. I'd much rather start a conversation by wetting my whistle."

Gabe's hand tightened on his holster. "And I'd rather start with a name."

The man shrugged. "Have it your way, gunslinger, but I'll have more to say if I wet my tongue first."

"I prefer to know who I'm drinking with."

"Fair enough." The man's grin widened as if he was pleased with what he was hearing. "I run my faro table under the name of Sharp Masterson."

"And your real name is?"

"Must you ask so many questions, gunslinger?"

"Most men prefer to keep me talking."

The man laughed aloud this time and reached for the drink Layla offered. Taking a sip, he eyed Gabe over the rim. "Colt Branson, since you insist on knowing."

Gabe shook his head. "Not ringing a bell. Don't suppose you go by any other handles?"

"Nope. I keep a low profile, but the second name I gave you is real enough."

The man's direct manner impressed Gabe as honest. It wasn't accompanied by the usual twitching and glancing away of a person with something to hide.

"I'm listening." Anxious to finish filling the clawing hole in his belly, he resumed eating his mutton pie with gusto. The sooner he finished eating, the sooner he could get moving again. He'd made many enemies in his line of business. As a rule, he never stayed too long in any one town.

Colt held his gaze with unwavering intensity. "As I said before, I need your help. More precisely, The Boomtown Mail Order Brides Company needs your help."

Boomtown what? Gabe waited a few heartbeats before attempting to swallow the bite of pie in his mouth. As it was, he had to choke it down and cough to clear his throat. If he had any laughter left in his soul, he would have laughed. "Clearly you're confused about what line of business I'm in, Mr. Branson."

The man waved his hand carelessly. "You can drop the mister. Just call me Colt. And you're exactly the kind of man I need for this job."

Gabe was only half listening as he finished up his last bite of pie and nursed the remaining swig or two of his ale. He swirled it around the bottom of his glass before taking a sip.

"We've lost contact with one of our brides-to-be."

Your problem. Not mine. Gabe raised his brows, incredulous that Colt had singled him out to share his sorry tale. Rescuing damsels in distress was a skill he simply didn't possess. Hot-Tempered Hannah was proof enough of that. A fresh splinter of pain ricocheted through his chest. He emptied his mug, hardly realizing he'd pressed a palm to his heart where his ache was the worse.

Colt's gaze followed his hand. "You and I both know the West isn't a safe place for young, marriageable women. Why so many of them flock to fill the ever-growing pile of mail order bride applications is thoroughly beyond me. Even the toughest among them don't always survive. Better to stay in more civilized cities back East."

Gabe wished the man would hurry up and get to his point. *Even the toughest...don't always survive.* The conversation was treading dangerously close to Hannah's tragic demise, making his trigger finger itch something powerful.

Colt abruptly shoved aside his dealer box to lean closer. He lowered his voice, but it accentuated rather than lessened the fierceness of his words. "My own sister, may she rest in peace, was one of those eager mail order brides. I'll never know why she decided to become one. Probably speculate myself into an early grave. Maybe it was because she wasn't much use with a needle and thread. Or maybe it was because anytime I caught her in the kitchen, I tended to skip dinner that night. But she could ride a horse like a demon, and she could hold her own with a gun." He shook his head admiringly, then sobered. "In the end, gunslinger, neither of those things could save MaryAnne from the cruelty of the man she married."

"What happened?" Gabe both wanted to know and didn't want to know.

"Her late husband claimed it was a stagecoach robbery that went south." He balled his hands into fists on the table-top. "Said they were in the wrong place at the wrong time, but that doesn't explain the fire or the—" He fiercely bit off whatever else he was about to say and took a deep breath. "The stage company was kind enough to send her remains home, so we could lay her to rest."

It was a tragic tale, yet Gabe found himself envying the man his closure. As for himself, he'd never received a body to bury, only the news that Hot-Tempered Hannah was dead. He bit down on the inside of his cheek. Hard. Enough to draw the coppery tang of blood across his tongue. "I'm sorry for your loss but with all due respect, I don't see how any of this applies to me." Harsh but true.

Colt's upper lip curled. "I don't believe that for a second. Don't tell me you've never asked your Maker for a do-over."

"A do-over?"

"A second chance."

Leave it alone, mister. Gabe's hand literally tingled with the itch to draw and fire. Colt Branson clearly had no idea what dangerous ground he was treading. "I have no idea what you're talking about."

"Of course, you do, and that's why you're going to help me find Heloise."

"Who?" Gabe choked back a snarl. Maybe the man was a bit touched in the head. It was the only explanation for his foolish persistence in toying with a gunslinger.

"She's one of our mail order brides. We should have received her letter by now, notifying us of her safe arrival to Headstone; but there've been no letters. No mention of her among the other brides we placed in neighboring towns. Nothing. She just—" He snapped his fingers. "Up and vanished!" His skin beneath his tan had paled, and he sounded truly distraught.

Gabe scrubbed a hand down his jaw, wishing he could offer a ray of comfort to the troubled faro dealer, touched in the noggin' or not. "Mail runs slow in some parts of the country. Maybe you should give it more time."

"We require our brides to write their letters before they leave Boston. All each of them has to do when she reaches her destination is date it and mail it."

"So have a chat with the post master."

For the first time in their short conversation, Colt's mouth gave an ugly downward twist of irritation. "Come on, gunslinger. I arrived here a week ago. Tracking down that fellow was the first thing on my list, and I was prepared to rip out his toenails one by one if need be to jog his memory of her. Except the poor chap seems to have vanished as well. I asked around town about him, but they said he was involved in some sort of stage coach accident. They found remnants of the carriage and wheels strewn down the side of a cliff but no bodies."

So the hopeful bride was missing. Tough times. She could be anywhere. Holed up in the mountains or chained inside a brothel, her virtue a distant memory. Anger churned in Gabe's gut. Unfortunately, things like that happened on occasion in the wild West. Some women just weren't meant to travel to these dusty towns of lonely, lust-crazed, and sometimes desperate men. Not everyone could hold their own or go out guns a-blazing like Hot-Tempered Hannah had.

Colt's missing Heloise was dead or as good as dead. Gabe wasn't a doomsday kind of guy; he was just facing the facts. Why then did questions start to bubble up his throat about the unfortunate woman?

"How long has she been missing, and what did she look like?" he blurted. Was she pretty enough to attract the attention of a madame? Had Colt bothered to scope out the brothels in the nearest towns?

He didn't know why he was asking. He certainly had no intention of helping Colt and his mail order bride company. Not for any price. He was too afraid of what he might find on the other end. The carnage. And death.

Too afraid of failing to save another woman.

Colt's shoulders relaxed a fraction at the barrage of questions, though his forearms remained resting on the edge of the table. The music in the background transitioned from a swinging ballad to something rowdier. The room grew louder. And hotter. And more suffocating.

Gabe could only pray he and Colt were about finished with their miserable discussion. Lord help him, he needed some fresh air.

"The last time any of us saw Heloise was two months ago when she boarded her train. She was wearing a simple brown taffeta gown." Colt's face settled into another half-grin. "When she first came to us, she had the kind of red hair no comb can tame, though the Boomtown matrons on our staff tried their best. They couldn't tame her mouth either. Or erase the bruises way down deep in her eyes. Impressed me as one of those wild little fillies who's seen things she didn't care to talk about. Our other brides-to-be tried to befriend her, but she mostly kept to herself. Kind of haunted like. Not that she would have fit in with them anyway." He gave a long, drown-out sigh of regret. "Reminded me of my sister, MaryAnne. She wasn't soft or gently spoken. Not skilled in any womanly arts that I could tell. She didn't look all that comfortable in a dress either, come to think of it. But she was full of fire no scoundrel has the right to put out before her time."

Colt's description of the young woman made Gabe swallow hard. Heloise sounded like Hot-Tempered Hannah all over again. A free spirit. An untamed heart with a thirst for adventure. And deader than dead if she'd already been missing for two full months.

There was no way Colt Branson could possibly know every one of his words sank into his listener like a gunshot. By the time the faro dealer was through describing his missing bride-to-be, it was all Gabe could do to remain sitting upright in his chair. His chest and torso were so riddled with emotional holes, he wouldn't have been the least shocked to feel the drip of blood on the hands he had fisted on his thighs.

Another woman was dead. It was an old, tired tale. Hell simply wasn't big enough for all the scum-eating renegades crawling the landscape these days. The gold-hungry, devil-may-care, barely human creatures who lived for little more than the next thrill. They were affection-starved and utterly depraved. Men who couldn't remember what it was like to be in the presence of a real lady. Men who wouldn't hesitate to take advantage of one, given half a chance.

"I'm sorry. I can't help you." Colt could shower his ears with all the piteous pleas in the world, but it wouldn't bring the missing bride one step closer to being found. It would be easier to locate a five-leaf clover in a field of December snow. Heloise was gone. The sooner Colt accepted the fact, the better.

"Can't or won't?" Colt snarled, gripping the edges of the table with both hands.

"Can't. Won't. Does it matter? She's gone." Gabe pushed away from the table and stood, desperate for a mouthful of fresh air before his lungs exploded.

"Is that what you want to believe?" Colt stood as well. "Because you buried your partner's body like I buried my sister's?"

How in tarnation did Colt know so much about his past when they'd never met before tonight? "Watch yourself, Sharp." Gabe's hand slid to his gun holster again. Hannah had been burnt alive; there had been nothing left to bury. Something told him Colt knew this, too.

"Did you?" Colt pressed. "Because if you did, then I'm wasting my breath by telling you the Boomtown Mail Order Brides Company received a ransom note for Heloise."

Meaning the poor woman might still be alive after all. And probably wishing she was dead...

"How much?" Gabe gritted through his teeth, making an inhuman effort to keep his voice down.

"Two grand."

It was a fortune. More than most lawmen made in a year and bigger than any other single bounty Gabe had earned. "Why so much?"

"Her abductor didn't say, but he seemed awfully concerned about listing every known name in the ransom note that Heloise might have ever used. Hester. Holly." He paused, dipping his head to peer beneath Gabe's Stetson. "Hannah."

For a moment, Gabe couldn't hear past the buzzing in his head. Hester and Holly were among the many aliases Hot-

Tempered Hannah had used on their string of joint assignments as bounty hunters.

"Oh, and here's the sketch another one of our mail order brides made of Heloise the night before she traveled West to meet her intended groom." Colt reached inside his vest and withdrew a charcoal portrait. He held it out.

Gabe reached for the small square of canvas and his insides went numb. He took a stumbling step towards the table and sank back into his seat. A coldness like he'd never known before spread through his chest. The sketch wasn't a perfect likeness, but it was close enough. There was no mistaking the challenging tilt of the woman's face or the determined set to her chin.

It was Hannah or someone who resembled her enough to pass as her twin, which made no sense. Hannah had never mentioned a sister. She'd never mentioned having family at all, for that matter.

The sketch slid from his nerveless fingers to the table. He slowly leaned forward on his elbows to grip his head in both hands. He closed his eyes, uncaring that his movements sent his Stetson tumbling to the floor. He fisted his hair roots until the tearing pressure on his skull rivaled the screaming questions in his brain.

There was another possibility — one that filled him with frantic joy and raging agony — that, by some miracle, Hannah was alive.

If it were true, it could only mean one thing. She'd faked her death. But why? Had she done it to double-cross him and take their final bounty purse for herself? Was it possible the woman he'd loved with every ounce of his life had secretly despised him in return? So much so that she'd been that desperate to get rid of him?

Gabe's heart felt like it was festering with a thousand blisters. The worst part about the possibility that Hannah was still alive was the fact she was trying to marry another man.

He didn't know how long he sat there. It could have been minutes or hours before the red-hot lava of anger finally burst through his numbness. Heat shot through his bloodstream and gave him the strength to lower his hands and meet Colt's concerned gaze. He needed answers. No, he desperately craved them, and there was only one way to get them. "I'm going to find her."

He would track her down, haul her double-crossing hide back to Headstone, and demand answers to every question scorching the walls of his soul. She owed him that at least.

"I know you will." Colt produced a folded parchment and slid it across the table in his direction. "Here's our contract. We'll cover your travel expenses, and there will be a sizable reward when you return her to us. Not anywhere near as big as the ransom note but enough to make it worth your while."

Gabe wasn't taking anyone's money. Not for this job. Finding Hannah was strictly personal. He started to crumple the contract, but Colt's eyelids narrowed to warning slits.

"You'll not lay eyes on the ransom note until you sign my contract."

The maniacal thought ran through Gabe's head that he could shoot Colt's knees out from under him and torture him into giving him what he wanted, but Colt didn't exactly impress him as a man who would buckle quickly or easily under pressure. And Gabe didn't have time to quibble. Heloise had already been missing two months. The clock was ticking.

When Colt handed him a pen, he scrawled a hasty signature. "Tell me everything you know."

"I will as soon as you raise your right hand and repeat your oath of allegiance to the Gallant Rescue Society."

Gallant who? Never mind. It didn't matter. Gabe's insides

churned with determination as he recited the oath, hardly registering the words coming from his mouth. "I hereby solemnly pledge my gun and my honor to the Gallant Rescue Society...so help me God."

Like a stallion pawing at the ground, he was frothing at the mouth to break into a gallop on his mission. The only thing in the world that mattered anymore was finding Hannah. He'd start his search in the Yellow Diamond Mine on the outskirts of Headstone. It was where she'd supposedly burnt to death during a premature dynamite explosion in an underground tunnel. A place of business he swore he'd never return to. The home of a gang of squatters who wanted him dead.

Hope you enjoyed the excerpt from
Mail Order Brides Rescue Series 1:
Hot-Tempered Hannah
Available now in eBook, paperback, and Kindle Unlimited on Amazon.

This is a complete 12-book series.
Read them all!
Book 1: Hot-Tempered Hannah
Book 2: Cold-Feet Callie
Book 3: Fiery Felicity
Book 4: Misunderstood Meg
Book 5: Dare-Devil Daisy
Book 6: Outrageous Olivia
Book 7: Jinglebell Jane
Book 8: Absentminded Amelia
Book 9: Bookish Belinda
Book 10: Tenacious Trudy

Book 11: Meddlesome Madge
Book 12: Mismatched MaryAnne
Box Set #1: Books 1-4
Box Set #2: Books 5-8
Box Set #3: Books 9-12

Much love,
Jovie

Also by Jovie

For the most up-to-date printable list of my sweet historical books:

Click here

or go to:

https://www.jografford.com/joviegracebooks

For the most up-to-date printable list of my sweet contemporary books:

Click here

or go to:

https://www.JoGrafford.com/books

About Jovie

Jovie Grace is an Amazon bestselling author of sweet and inspirational historical romance books full of faith, family, and second chances. She also writes sweet contemporary romance as Jo Grafford.

1.) Follow on Amazon!
https://www.amazon.com/author/joviegrace

2.) Join Cuppa Jo Readers!
https://www.facebook.com/groups/CuppaJoReaders

3.) Follow on Bookbub!
https://www.bookbub.com/authors/jovie-grace

4.) Follow on Facebook!
https://www.facebook.com/JovieGraceBooks

Made in the USA
Las Vegas, NV
13 March 2024

87173159R00114